The Fear Man

ALSO BY ANN HALAM
The Haunting of Jessica Raven

The Fear Man

Ann Halam

Orion
Children's Books

For Herta Ryder, my dear friend

First published in Great Britain in 1995
by Orion Children's Books
a division of the Orion Publishing Group Ltd
Orion House
5 Upper St Martin's Lane
London WC2H 9EA

A catalogue record of this book is available from the British Library

Typeset by Deltatype Ltd, Ellesmere Port, Cheshire
Printed in England by Clays Ltd, St Ives plc

ISBN 1 85881 158 9

One

*I*T BEGAN ON A DULL, COLD DAY AT THE END OF WINTER.
It was a Saturday. We'd been shopping – me, my
Mum, my sister Elsa and my brother Max. Mum needed
some office supplies for her phone sales job, so we went
looking for a proper stationery shop. We ended up streets
away from our usual beat, way out on Roman Road. We'd
lived in the area for months, far the longest that we'd
stayed in one place since Dad died. (I thought of him as
Dad, though he was Elsa and Max's father, not mine.) But
I didn't remember having been on this road before. I knew
the name because I'd seen a shabby old black and white
sign up on the side of a building. It was one of those big,
dirty, city rat-tracks where nobody wants to live any more.
There were no pubs; the few shops you could see were
metal-grilled or boarded up; and the traffic roared by,
never pausing. The houses were grimy and battered; some
of them seemed half derelict. The one beside us looked as if
it had been empty for years.

Mum had stopped suddenly – from sheer tiredness, I
supposed. We'd been trudging around for ages. The
buggy was loaded up with shopping. I was in charge of it.
Mum was holding Max by the hand; he was grizzling
because he was cold. Elsa and I were used to situations like
this, but he'd just turned three and he wasn't much of a
tough. He was whimpering *I want to go home* over and over
again. I could tell it was getting to Mum. She stood staring
at the empty house, biting her lip, and then glanced up and
down the road anxiously. I knew she was thinking that
people were watching us, though there was no one in sight.

I also knew, from experience, that there was nothing I could do or say. If I let on that I'd noticed she was feeling bad, I'd make things worse.

'Is there something wrong, Mummy?' asked Elsa.

'Nothing . . .' said Mum. 'Nothing's wrong. Look. There's a bus stop. Let's go home.'

'What about the shop you were looking for?' I didn't want to hassle her, but it would be worse if we got home and she suddenly remembered she was short of something.

'It'll wait. Come on, *let's go*. Give me the pushchair.'

She grabbed the buggy handles from me, managed to stow the whingeing Max in among our carrier bags, and set off back the way we'd come. I was about to follow her, when I noticed that Elsa was still staring at the empty house. The stop was only fifty metres away, and there wasn't a bus in sight. I thought it wouldn't do any harm to let Mum have a couple of minutes on her own.

The house stood back from the pavement, behind a low wall with an iron railing on top of it. There was a wrought iron gate between brick pillars. Behind it, steps led down to a basement entrance that was out of sight from the road, and up to the front door. A tree had taken root in the sloping patch of earth in the basement area and grown up past the ground-floor windows. Its bare twigs reached and tapped on the dark glass. At the base of the wall a thick mulch of rubbish had gathered: sweet wrappers, squashed cans, old take-away cartons, scraps of newspaper, all mingled in a dusty stew. Elsa was standing in this gunk, gazing intently through the railings.

'What are you looking at?'

'The house,' said my sister calmly.

I stared at it with her. I thought I'd rarely seen a house that looked so *dead*. It was like a road-killed rabbit that someone had kicked into the verge, lying there unburied and slowly sinking into the dirt. I could imagine how damp and dark it would be in those rooms behind the tree branches. In the front hall there'd be a pile of mouldy junk mail. When you shoved the door open, a chill smell of murk and decay would waft out to meet you. I knew about houses like this. Since Dad died and we'd been on the move, we'd had to take whatever accommodation we could find: hard-to-rent flats with fungus on the kitchen walls, places that were barely habitable. But an empty house always has a kind of promise. I knew that Elsa was thinking the same as me – that we'd like to get inside and spook around the empty rooms, poke in the cupboards, maybe find some treasure or mystery there. However, the house might not even be empty. There was a rag of yellow lace curtain in one upstairs window, and someone had been using the gate recently. You could see the mark it had grooved in the rubbish on the path inside.

'Maybe it's haunted,' I suggested.

'I know it is, Andrei,' answered Elsa, 'This is definitely a haunted house.'

Elsa was seven and a half that winter, and I was fourteen. But she wasn't exactly a normal seven-year-old. The life we'd led had made her into a strange mixture, believing in childish things like ghosts and magic, but somehow not in a childish way. I was never sure how to take it; was she serious or not? I didn't want to encourage her, so I moved over to examine the pillars on either side of the gate. They had been faced with something to make them look like stone. The stuff had flaked away in raggedy scales like cement dandruff. I picked up a sharp-edged piece and started to scrape at the capstone on the left-hand pillar. The way the crust of dirt came off, like a scab from a cut, made me feel slightly sick. But it was something to do.

'What are you poking at?'

'There's some lettering here; I want to find out what it says.'

I scraped out an 'R' and part of an 'E' – or maybe an 'L' –

and then an 'F'. The rest was gone beyond recall. I moved over to the other post, and had better luck. 'N,' I said, digging out the grooves. 'O . . . C . . .' I suddenly had a feeling that someone in the house was watching me. I looked up. I could have sworn I saw that old lace curtain twitch.

'You shouldn't do that. You might activate something.'

The curtain didn't move again. I gave up my excavation, because I'd spotted a rather weird object lying in the grunge. It was a lump about the size of a hen's egg, but fleshy dark pink and slightly nubbly, like a human tongue. It looked like a piece of some animal's insides. Maybe somebody had dropped a raw kidney or a chicken heart here on the way back from the butcher's. But it looked stranger than that, and even more disgusting.

Elsa came to look. 'Don't touch it,' she said. 'I think that's a guarding device.'

'*What?*'

'A kind of magic burglar alarm,' she explained, as if she knew all about it. 'A guarding device is when you make something that keeps watch when you're not there. Don't touch it. You shouldn't even look at it for long, or you'll set off the alarm.'

Sometimes I felt I had to made a stand against Elsa's weirdness, so I deliberately poked the chicken-heart egg with the toe of my shoe. It rolled a little, and came to rest against a decayed fragment of hamburger carton. Nothing happened. But I'd leaned against the gate, and it swung open. Elsa and I looked at each other with the same thought.

'Well, you've done it now,' she whispered. 'We might as well go in.'

I glanced down the road. Mum and Max were sitting on the bench inside the bus shelter. I couldn't hear but I could see that Max was talking to her. They looked all right. It was getting late. There was a shadow in the daylight, a still, cold, waiting-for-darkness feel in the air. There was nobody in sight except for Mum and Max. And there was no sign of a bus looming over the horizon. I shrugged.

'Okay, just for a minute.'

It was almost as if the house had invited us.

The dirt on the front steps was caked hard. It didn't give underfoot. I was glad we wouldn't leave footprints. I tried to peer through the windows, but it was too dark in there. I could only see the branches of the tree reflected in the glass. Elsa inspected the front door. There was a blackened metal number: 2121, and a letterbox with a brass knocker attached that had become congealed to the frame. There was a door knob too. I thought of trying it, to see if the door was locked. But of course it must be.

'Shall we knock?' I said, joking. The house was surely empty. Close up, it was more *dead* than ever, and creepy as an abandoned graveyard. The impulse that had brought me through the gate had vanished. But since we were here, I had to do something. I pushed the flap of the letterbox. It gave crustily: I bent down and peered in.

'What can you see?' demanded Elsa.

There was the gloomy, narrow hall. A pile of junk mail and old newspapers lay festering on the floor, just as I'd imagined it. There was another of those chicken-heart egg things, lying on the damp envelopes. At first I thought I might be mistaken. The hall was pretty gloomy. But I've always had good night vision. I could see the pinkish lump clearly. Then I thought I saw it move. I jumped. The flap snapped shut.

'What did you see? *What did you see?*'

'Nothing. This is stupid.' I couldn't believe I'd really seen what I thought I saw. 'Come on, out of it, Elsa. We're trespassing.'

She gave me one of her looks – the eye-rolling, disgusted-old-lady expression – and shoved the letterbox open.

'What did you see that scared you, Andrei? You'd better tell me.'

'I wasn't *scared*,' I protested.

By now I wanted to look again, to find out if the chicken-heart thing actually *was* there. I wanted to know if it really had moved, jerking and shifting as if something was hatching out of it. I tried to push Elsa out of the way. She hung on. For a moment we were fighting over the narrow viewpoint, then Elsa screamed.

She screamed again, and shot backwards from the door. I grabbed her. We belted down the rubbish-strewn steps and leapt through the gate as if hordes of monsters were chasing us. It was fun, to tell you the truth. My heart was actually pounding as I dragged the gate shut behind me. I didn't really believe that Elsa and I had disturbed the bogeyman, so I wasn't *afraid*. It was just a thrill. The next moment, I wished I'd kept my head. Mum was there at the gate, clinging to Max and looking horrified.

'What have you done?' she cried. 'Andrei! What have you done?'

I knew how her mind would be working. She wasn't afraid of spooks. She was afraid of *attracting attention*, as she called it. She could never forget that she didn't belong in this country. She was convinced that if any of us got into any kind of trouble, we'd be thrown out.

'It's okay,' I told her quickly. 'We didn't do anything wrong. We weren't trying to break in. We were only fooling around. The place is empty.'

Mum stared at the house in a panic. I was afraid some decrepit old codger would appear after all, and dodder out, indignant, to demand who was making all the row. Luckily nothing happened.

'Let's go,' she muttered. 'We can't wait for the bus. It's not safe.'

So we walked all the way home. We managed to get lost twice. Max refused to walk, and the buggy couldn't hold him and our bags for any distance, so we had to carry all the shopping. Elsa kept trying to catch my eye. I knew she wanted to persuade me that we'd genuinely seen a ghost. I wasn't having any of it. As soon as I could get her alone, I planned to tell her off for screaming like that. She knew as well as I did what Mum was like.

We were living in a quiet little street fairly near the Common, our local park. We had a whole house, with three bedrooms and a garden at the back. It was by far the nicest place we'd lived in for years. We'd never have got hold of it, except that it had been a short let to start with, too short for people with settled lives. It had turned out that the owners didn't want to sell the place after all, or move into it themselves. So they'd gone on renting it to us.

I didn't have a chance to get hold of Elsa until after tea, when Mum was putting Max to bed. It was dark by then, and our living room was cosy, with the curtains drawn and the tv chattering to itself in the corner. Elsa had settled down to do some drawing, her favourite occupation, but she knew I was after her. As soon as Mum took off to give Max his bath, she gathered up her stuff and scooted. I collared her in the doorway before she could escape upstairs.

'I want to talk to you. *What did you scream like that for? Are you crazy?* You know what's going to happen, don't you, if Mum starts getting nervous again –'

She knew. It had happened often enough. We would find somewhere to live. Mum would get us into schools, and get herself some work she could do at home. We'd start to relax – and then something would go wrong. Some little thing would start Mum off. She'd tell us she was being followed, that the neighbours were spying on us, that the teachers at our schools were asking questions, that it wasn't safe to stay . . . And we'd be uprooted again.

—— 7 ——

Elsa glared at me. 'I did not scream.'

'Don't be daft. You did. Okay, it was fun. We were playing a game, pretending that the house was haunted. But you didn't have to scream like that.'

'You screamed too. And you started it. You opened the gate.'

This was a complete lie. It had opened by itself. 'I did not start anything! Look, Elsa, all I'm saying is watch out. I don't want to move again. I like my school. I like it here.'

She let me finish, but she wasn't paying attention. 'I don't know exactly what you've started, Andrei, but I'm afraid we're in for trouble.' She changed her tone and called sweetly up the stairs, 'Can I come to bed early, Mum? I'm tired. I'll read Max his story if you like.'

She whisked out of my grip, leaving me fuming.

Mum and I watched the tv and talked a bit. She didn't mention the empty house or Elsa's screaming fit. Maybe that was odd, because it was very unusual for Elsa to be scared of anything, but I didn't think of it at the time. I watched Mum doing her accounts. We had hardly any money, but she was incredibly careful not to get into debt. It was one of her many terrors. Every so often she paused to sip her vitamin-juice supper. Mum never ate meals with us. She picked at food like a bird. Sometimes she hardly seemed to eat anything – all part of her bad nerves. She looked up and caught my eye.

'We're doing all right,' she said, smiling. She propped her chin on one hand, and rubbed the other through her cropped hair. My Mum's a small woman, with black hair, black eyes, and a white skin that never tans. 'You like it here Andrei, don't you?'

'I do,' I said. 'I hope we don't have to move again. You seem happier too.'

I dared to say that, because until this afternoon's trek to Roman Road, she had seemed much better – better than I'd known her to be since Dad died. She'd been desperate when that happened. It was sudden, he was killed in a car crash when Max was still just a baby, and Mum fell apart. I'd seen her in some terrible states – afraid to leave the house, crying all the time, completely helpless – I'd seen it all. I was the only one who'd been there. Mum never went to a doctor, never asked for any kind of help. She thought those people, *the authorities*, were all the same. She wouldn't go near them.

When I was very young, I used to be scared of them too. I used to lie awake when I was hardly older than Max, wondering what on earth I'd do if *they* came to throw us in prison or send us away; and if they'd take Beano, my teddy bear, away from me. Nowadays, I was old enough to know that there was nothing wrong with Mum's 'papers'. No one could pack her up and dump her back in the dreaded 'old country'. But she couldn't believe it. She'd been afraid too long.

However, just now she seemed to have recovered from whatever had made her panic. 'You've put up with a lot from me, Andrei, haven't you? Well, don't worry. I've sorted myself out. I'm going to make our life work this time.'

She put the bills and receipts away, and picked up a circular Elsa had brought home from school. 'Have you seen this? It's about the Community Fun Day they have on the Common in June. There's a parade, and live music, and stalls. It sounds like fun. They're asking for helpers. You know, I think I might go to their meeting.'

I was so amazed at this that I didn't dare comment.

We watched some more tv, and then we went to bed. Or rather I went to bed and Mum went to her room. She's a nocturnal animal. She cat-naps during the day and never sleeps more than a few hours at a time. Max had shared a room with Elsa since he was a baby, so that Mum could read and fidget about without disturbing him. As I crawled into bed, exhausted by all that trudging, I was wondering –

without taking the idea seriously – what kind of 'trouble' Elsa expected. I found out, at about midnight.

I woke, not sure what had woken me. I lay staring at the familiar furniture of my room, each angle neatly outlined in the darkness. Good old Beano was sitting in my chair as usual, with a sock perched on his head. I wondered how that got there . . . I was wide awake, and the night was tingling with danger. I knew that something had happened. I slipped out of bed, dead silent, and pulled on a sweater (I sleep in an old tracksuit; I don't like pyjamas). There was no light under Mum's door, all was quiet. I went into the kids' room. Max was standing up in his cot, clinging to the bars. Elsa was by the window.

'What is it?' I breathed.

'Come and look. Don't move the curtains. Look through the gap . . .'

At the back of our house the windows were the old-fashioned sash cord kind. They weren't very secure and Mum worried about them. But the kids' bedroom window was a good ten or twelve metres off the ground, and there wasn't an easy way into the narrow gardens that faced each other, back-to-back between two rows of houses. We were reasonably safe from intruders. I looked out, and saw our little back garden lying quiet and dim. There was a scattering of still-lit windows in the houses around, but mostly the darkness was undisturbed.

'I can't see anything.'

'*Look on the wall.*'

I saw something greyish plastered against the dark bricks. I couldn't make out what it was at first – not because I couldn't see, but because the shape seemed to waver. Then it steadied, and I saw the skeletal grey limbs, the long fingers clinging. The thing turned up its face, and looked at me . . .

Max scrambled out of his cot and came to join us. We

stood there staring. Max got hold of my hand and Elsa's. He was trembling, but he didn't make a sound.

'It wants to get in,' whispered Elsa. 'What shall we do?'

I had seen this creature before, or something like it. I had seen it uncoiling and boiling out from a fleshy, rubbery pink egg, on the door mat of the empty house. I knew this, but I couldn't believe it. I watched, hypnotised. It moved like a stick insect. It was easing itself across the wall and climbing at the same time. It had looked up, right at this window. We'd seen the eyes and nostrils and gaping mouth like holes in a paper mask, like the face of a sad grey clown. But I didn't think it had seen us.

'I'll deal with it.'

I unfastened the catch and opened the window as quietly as I could. When I looked down the thing on the wall was still slowly, carefully groping the bricks. I stuck my leg over the sill and reached for the drainpipe.

'Andrei!' hissed Elsa.

It had seen me. It dropped, into the dark.

'Oh, Andry,' cried Max, his anxious face just visible over the edge of the windowsill. 'Poor man, maybe it wants to be our pet. Don't hurt it. Don't kill it or peuw it!'

Peuw meant shoot or zap, like in a video game. My brother Max is the softest-hearted child I have ever met. 'It's okay, Maxie. I'm not carrying a gun.'

I swung on to the drainpipe, scrambled down and dropped on to our patch of lawn. I looked around. Was I afraid? Maybe I was scared to death, but I was reacting, not thinking. Where had the thing gone? There wasn't a sound from Max and Elsa above. There wasn't a sound anywhere except for the distant roar of traffic, and a tinny jabbering from someone's late-night tv. I imagined stick-insect, skeleton arms suddenly grabbing my neck from behind . . . Nothing grabbed me. I looked right and left: I couldn't see any sign of it. It must have escaped.

Then movement caught my eye. There was something

grey, writhing and flailing against our left-hand neighbours' fence. I took a step towards the monster. It didn't see me, it seemed absorbed in its own horrible contortions, and somehow its blind, senseless movements were more scary than anything. Sweat broke out all over me. My mind had caught up now, and I was truly afraid. Then I laughed.

The monster was a heap of old newspaper.

I pulled it off the fence, bundled it together, and stuck the lot in our wheelie bin. I started to laugh again. An old newspaper! How ridiculous!

I crept back to the window and called up. 'Elsa!'

'What happened?'

'Nothing. It wasn't anything, just a piece of old newspaper. Go into my room, fetch my keys from my jacket pocket and throw them down. And get Max back into bed.'

She brought the keys. I caught them, and quietly let myself in by the back door. I crept upstairs. It was strange how silent the house was. As I reached the top step, I thought I saw something move. A black shadow – darkness on darkness – seemed to pass across the open door of the kids' room. I yelled out loud, fell backwards, grabbed the stair rail, and landed with a thump, the edge of a step connecting painfully with my back. Mum's door opened.

'What's all the banging and yelling? Is there something wrong, Andrei?'

The shadow had vanished, of course. 'Nothing,' I said. 'I went to fetch a book for Elsa. She insisted on going to bed early, and now she says she can't sleep. Then I fell downstairs. I've merely broken some ribs; no problem.'

Mum chuckled. 'Okay. G'night.'

I told the kids what I'd found, and ordered them back to bed.

Elsa wasn't satisfied. She was determined to believe in the ghost. I refused to argue with her in the middle of the night. In the morning I took her to look in the wheelie bin. Unfortunately, this was after breakfast. Mum had emptied a heap of kitchen rubbish in there and we couldn't see the crumpled newspaper. I knew I'd shoved it in there. Elsa couldn't convince me otherwise. I remembered the disgusting slimy feel of decayed newsprint. But I refused to tip out the bin and root through the whole mess, just to show her. I pointed out that there were no footprints except mine on the lawn, which was soft and muddy.

'That proves nothing. Ghosts don't leave footprints.'

'You are crazy!' I thought of the empty clown-face staring up at us in the dark, and shuddered. 'Don't you realise how horrible an actual ghost would be? Infants love horror stories. You can't help it, it's in your genes. But you sound as if you want it to be true.'

'I'm not an infant. And I don't *want* it to be true. I'm facing the facts.'

'Don't be silly. An old newspaper flapped up against the house, blown by the wind –'

'There was no wind.'

'What . . . ? Of course there was. There was a wind earlier . . .' I remembered, suddenly, how still the garden had been. 'There must have been a wind.'

Elsa shook her head. 'You know there wasn't. You haven't asked me yet why Max and I woke up. You know the ghost didn't make any noise.'

I heaved a patient sigh. 'Okay, why did you wake up? Not that I'll believe you, whatever story you tell me.'

'It called us,' she said simply. 'It called our names – Max and Elsa. I expect, if you think about it, you'll remember that it called you, too.'

'Andrei' . . . *I had woken in the dark, and someone, a voice I didn't know but almost recognised, had been calling my name.* She was right.

I couldn't believe it. I wouldn't admit it.

'There's something in that house on Roman Road,' said

Elsa gravely. 'It's out to get us. And *you opened the gate.* You shouldn't have done that. Why don't you listen, when I tell you things about magic?'

I felt like asking her, *what do you know about magic, anyway?* But I didn't care about Elsa's make-believe. I simply resented the whole business, particularly the way Elsa, having decided to believe her own scary story, made out it was all my fault.

'I did not open the gate. It opened by itself.'

Elsa shrugged. 'Tell that to the ghost.' She frowned. 'I'll have to do something. I've been thinking of a spell. Do you know where the street-map book is?'

'I'm not going to help you,' I said firmly.

'Yes you are. If you don't, I'll tell Mum that a ghost nearly climbed in through our window. She'll probably have a complete nervous breakdown.'

That's the kind of sister I had. I grabbed her arms, digging in hard so it would hurt.

'Don't you *dare* tell Mum about this!' I snarled. 'Or I'll tear you apart!'

Elsa looked at me scornfully. 'Mum knows more than you think. *She* was scared of the house too. Didn't you notice that? I did. Sometimes you're so *stupid.*'

Well, I decided to get her the street maps, to keep her quiet. We had a whole collection of them. They were stacked on a shelf in the dining-nook: a record of the towns and cities we'd passed through. As I looked through them I felt shivery prickles of anxiety. I remembered Mum standing by the empty house, looking so frightened. Elsa was right. She'd taken us off our usual beat, pretending to look for a shop we never found, and then she had begun to be afraid. Why? *Was* it something to do with that house? I didn't believe Elsa's ghost story; of course I didn't. But I sensed the beginning of a familiar pattern.

I gave Elsa the book and went with her to our corner shop. She asked Mrs Khan to enlarge a page, and make six copies of the enlargement. Guess who financed this operation, and Mrs Khan – who thought Elsa was wonderful – gave the brat a marshmallow chew for being so cute. We went home and fetched Max and the buggy, and set out for a long Sunday stroll, while Mum had a nap. I soon lost interest in the spell-casting. I was cold and uneasy, and I couldn't stop thinking about Mum. *Mum fixing on that empty house, the way I'd seen her fix on places before; Mum getting more and more scared* . . . Oh, no, I thought. It's starting again. Another city, another school, another street-map book for the collection. I did notice that Elsa's route was tracing a rough circle. We walked to the Common and then set off by way of the library; the High Street where we did our shopping; Elsa's school, where Max went to the nursery; the Monument where all the buses gathered – and back again to the Common, to the children's playground on the edge of the bare, windswept expanse of turf. Several times Elsa stopped, and marked something on the maps.

Max was thoroughly miserable by the time we reached the Common again. We had to spend about an hour in the playground, to make up for trailing him round the streets. All the Sunday fathers were reading their newspapers on the benches. The children – who'd been sent out for some contact time with Dad – were trying to kill each other on the slide and the jungle gym, while the dads read on, oblivious. It was a depressing place.

Elsa was very secretive about her spell after that. I knew she'd hidden the copied maps in different places around the house, because I found one, folded up small and stuffed into a crack under the bathroom windowsill. And I noticed that going outdoors had become shrouded in ritual. We could only reach the library or the Common by her special route, and we had to let the children stop, holding hands and shutting their eyes, on certain street corners. But this was a typical Elsa-game. Mum and I were used to humouring her, and thought nothing of it. (If you think we shouldn't have let a little girl order us about, all I can say is, you haven't met my sister.) I hoped she would forget about it in a few days, and Mum need never know how it had begun.

It was Friday, teatime, when she found out. Something good-smelling was cooking in the oven in the kitchen. (My mum doesn't eat much, but she's a fine cook). There were cartoons on the tv. Mum was doing paperwork for her sales job. I was reading homework. Max and Elsa were crouched over Elsa's drawing book, felt tips and crayons spread over the floor around them. I had spotted, from the corner of my eye, that one of Elsa's anti-ghost maps was hidden inside the book. I hoped Mum wouldn't see it. But my luck ran out. She pushed aside her work and said what a convenient job it was. You could work from home and nobody bothered you. She went to see what the children were doing.

'What are you drawing, babies?'

Though Elsa was so grown up, in her odd way, she loved it when Mum called her 'baby'. She snuggled into the curve of Mum's arm. I saw her sneakily pushing the street map out of sight.

'It's a secret,' said Elsa.

'Okay, I promise I won't tell anyone.'

Mum picked up the drawing book. I glimpsed a picture of a grey, gruesome, stick-limbed creature. It was viciously stuck through with spears or arrows, so it looked like an anorexic porcupine. The street map fell out on to the floor.

'What's this?' asked Mum, casually.

I glared at Elsa, and mouthed at her, over Mum's head, *I'll kill you!*

I think she got the message. I don't think she meant to spill the beans. We both knew better than to tell Mum anything that might make her fears worse. But she was only seven, after all. She lost her head.

'It's a magic map,' she blurted. 'It's to stop the ghost from getting us. You know, the ghost from the empty house.'

Mum stared at my sister, and then at the piece of paper. I read the same sentence in my textbook about fifteen times, or that's what it felt like. Elsa went pink and Max – sensing trouble – reverted to infanthood and started to cry. Mum put the map down carefully, as if it might explode. She pulled Max on to her knees and cuddled him.

'A spell against the ghost . . . That's a smart idea. Keep up the good work, Elsa.'

But her smile was thin and tense and jagged, like a scratch on glass.

After we'd eaten and washed up and the kids were in bed, I tried to escape to my room. She pinned me down. 'Andrei,' she said. 'What's this about a ghost?' She had me cornered against the table, and she was holding that pesky map.

'Mum, you know what happened. We were looking for a shop you wanted, the Saturday before last. You decided to give up, and went to wait for a bus. Elsa looked through the letterbox of an empty house, and pretended she'd seen a ghost. *That's all.* She and Max have made up a game about it—'

Mum was even whiter than usual, and there were pinched marks round her nose and mouth. 'The house on Roman Road,' she murmured. She looked at me hard. 'You haven't been back there, have you?'

'No. Why should I?'

She bit her lip. 'Andrei, you haven't seen anyone hanging around our place?'

'No!'

'You haven't noticed anyone watching you, on the street? Anyone following you?'

I felt sick. It was starting again, the same familiar

pattern. 'No, Mum. Honestly, it's all right. Please don't worry. It's nothing but a silly game.'

She nodded, slowly. 'Okay. But . . . if you notice *anything* unusual, you'll tell me?'

'Of course I will,' I lied. 'But there's nothing. We're safe here. We're settled. You even went to the Community Fun Day Meeting—'

This was true, and amazing. She had gone out by herself, leaving me to babysit.

'What?' She looked puzzled. 'Oh yes, that . . .'

Her words trailed away. She stared at the map again, shook her head and put it aside. Then she switched the tv to a different channel and I went off to my room. I managed to snag the street map on my way out, so I could get a good look at it. I didn't learn much. Elsa had drawn a circle around our house, and everywhere a street cut through her circle she'd blocked it off with a cross, a black cross with jags on it like tiny thorns. That was all.

When I was six years old, my mother took me out one night to see the stars. We were on holiday, the three of us, in a cottage in the country. I think it must have been our first holiday together: me and Mum and Alan, my new dad. I wasn't asleep when she came. I was dozing, listening to the country silence, and watching the delicate shadows of leaves on my white-washed ceiling. It was all strange to me, Mum and I had always lived in towns. I heard someone call my name. I went and looked out of the open window, and there was my mother standing in the grass below.

'Come out, Andrei. Come and join me.'

The cottage stood in a garden. There was a tree outside my window, the same one whose leaves made shadows on my ceiling. I felt as if I was asleep and dreaming. I didn't think of getting dressed or going downstairs. I climbed into the tree, and scrambled down to the ground. I skinned my knee on the way and it hurt, so I knew I must be awake.

'What's the matter?' I asked, holding her hand tight.

'Nothing's the matter. I wanted you to see the stars.'

She was wearing a beautiful dark blue spangly shawl over her teeshirt and jeans. It had belonged to her grandmother. Her grandmother's things were the only mementos she had kept from 'the old country' – that place I'd never seen, where Mum was once a child like me. Her voice sounded softer and clearer than it did by day, and her eyes were shining.

We walked away from the house. The long grass was wet. It felt good under my bare feet, but my pyjamas were getting soaked. I asked my mother if it had been raining, and she explained to me about dewfall: how the little drops of water form and fall out of the air when it cools after a long hot day. She showed me the green blink of a glow-worm in the hedge, and told me how the female bug flashes her light to attract a mate. We crouched down and I saw a little wingless grub clinging to a grass blade, her tail-section a blob of green light. We left her in peace to wait for her date, and went out into the lane. My mother moved with a swing in her step, as if she was dancing or about to take off and fly. The creepers hanging from the hedges were full of sweet scent; it was like walking past a perfume counter. She told me that was honeysuckle and wild roses. We didn't walk far. We came to a gate in the hedge, where the sky was clear above. She told me the names of some constellations, and tried to get me to repeat them back to her. I couldn't. She laughed and said it didn't matter.

'Whatever you call them,' she said, 'every part of you, every elemental atom in every molecule in your body, was made in the heart of a star. We're all the same in that.'

We stared up until our necks got sore. Then she lifted me down from the gate. She put her shawl round my shoulders and stroked her fingers along the insides of my arms. It made me shiver. 'That's where your blood comes from,' she said. 'Starlight runs in your veins.'

'Didn't Daddy want to see the stars?' I asked.

'Not tonight. Tonight is for you and me.'

It had been a worrying time. I definitely wanted us to be a real family, and I loved my dad. He'd been my friend from the first day we met. But I'd been afraid too. I wouldn't have dared to say so, I desperately didn't want to spoil anything, but I was afraid of losing her. Mum must have known that. Years later, I realised that our magic walk under the stars had been one of her ways of reassuring me, that nothing could come between us.

It became a family tradition. Mum had Elsa, and then Max. She didn't have as much time for me, and I was growing up and getting independent. But on holiday, wherever we were, in the country or by the sea, Mum and I would go out for walks in the dark to stare at the stars and the moon, and catch the wildlife going about its business. We'd come back and tell Dad we'd seen an owl hunting, or a hedgehog snuffling along with her babies. He'd laugh at us, and say it was warmer indoors. We sometimes went out 'stargazing' in the city too. There weren't many stars to be seen, but it didn't matter.

I didn't learn to recognise a lot of constellations. I still can't understand how people ever imagined they could see those join-the-dots lions and monsters and so forth. But I never forgot the magic of that first time, when she told me I was made from the heart of a star. One day, I found out it is the literal truth. The heavy elements that make up organic life, including our bodies, were formed, millions and millions of years ago, inside ancient stars that died and scattered their substance through the universe. I was amazed when I found that out, and slightly disappointed. That night when I was six, I'd thought it was my mum and me who were special, the star-children.

After Dad died the night walks stopped. We didn't have

holidays, and anyway, Mum wouldn't leave Max and Elsa on their own, night or day. She didn't trust babysitters. But sometimes I'd remember her the way she was that night. My beautiful mother, walking fearlessly in the dark, talking about atoms and molecules – words you'd never think she'd heard of, if you met her now. And I'd think of her the way she was these days, cowed and nervous and beaten-down, haunted by cruel fears. It was sad. But what could I do?

Two

*A*FTER SEEING MUM'S REACTION TO ELSA'S MAP, I WAS seriously worried. I decided to tell Dita about it, after school one day at Agnelli's.

Agnelli's had once been an ordinary fish and chip shop, with a café attached. The current owner was an Italian called Salvatore Rizzio. His wife Sunny, and her Hindu mother, had done a major culinary takeover. They still served fish and chips, but also did ace Hindu and South Indian food plus (which was what I liked best) Indian-style tea and coffee – thick and sweet and milky and frothy; and flavoured with spices if you wanted. The café had become the best place to eat and hang out in our part of town. It was very popular with the coolest boys in our fourth and fifth year, the likes of Vijay Kumar and Ashok Manaj and their fans. They filled the tables at lunchtimes, evenings, weekends; playing cards, talking loud, showing off their film-star profiles. I was distinctly low-life in here as a newbie and a non-Asian. But the smart-pack tolerated me because of Dita. She was the one who had told me Agnelli's background. She knew everything about our neighbourhood.

Dita was my best friend at school, I liked her a lot, though she was totally different from me. I'd met her the first week I arrived, when she spotted me getting some aggravation from the mean and nasty element in our year – and barged straight in to sort things out. That was like Dita. I believed in keeping my head down, no matter what. She was *wild*. You could never tell what Dita Mukarjee would do next. *She* never had any problems with the bullies – and neither did I after we became friends. But usually her mind was on higher things. Dita was the one who had organised the anti-pollution demo in my first term. She personally sabotaged all the staff cars – especially the big ones with dirty engines – with nuts and bolts and bits of can fixed in inaccessible places, so that when the teachers started up to drive home, it sounded like a metal earthquake . . .

The day I decided to tell her about my mum was the day she'd come off a fast-unto-death for her Animal Welfare campaign. She'd stuck it for three days solid, taking only water. It had been a whole-school scandal. Everyone had been talking about Dita, and passing round Compassion In World Farming leaflets and mailshots from the RSPCA. Mrs Preston, Mind Police Chief, aka our deputy head, had been making evil threats that Dita should *be taken somewhere for treatment.* The staff were going nuts, Dita's long-suffering parents were trying to keep things calm, and everyone in our year was hoping Dita would get us on tv. But she had suddenly decided that her fast wasn't right. So here she was, staring at a hearty snack plate of masala dosa and chips. (In case you didn't know, masala dosa is a lentil-flour pancake served with potato and onion gravy. You eat it with coconut chutney and it is *excellente.* Especially accompanied by Salvatore's superb chips.)

'It's no use,' she sighed. 'I can't stop people from being cruel by not eating. All I was doing was upsetting Mummy and Daddy. I'm a failure. I'm a pest, I wish I was dead.'

People found it hard to get annoyed with Dita, even people like Mrs Preston, because she was never showing off. Whatever the stunt was, she meant it, sincerely. And she was always honestly sorry about the trouble she caused.

'Eat your dosa,' I told her. 'You'll feel better. And you're *not* a failure. You got people talking. People respect you, Dita, because you believe in things. I know they do.'

'Everyone thinks I'm mad,' she said gloomily. She wiped away a tear that was trickling down her nose. 'You're supposed to break a fast on some fruit, or maybe a little strained yoghurt . . .' She thought about this, but the chips were tempting. She tucked in.

I was drinking sticky coffee with lots of hot milk. I couldn't really afford to eat in here.

'Anyway, I'm glad you've finished your fast. I want to tell you something serious.'

Dita stopped in the act of dipping a large fat chip into her coconut chutney.

'Good or bad?'

'Not so good, I think I might be leaving school.'

The part I hated most was the first interview at a new place. The head teacher or pastoral deputy or whoever would already have looked at my records. Single-parent family; mother in no-qualifications job; absenteeism. (There were times when I *had to* stay at home, to look after Mum as much as to mind Max and Elsa.) Other children in the family with a different father; always moving; disrupted schooling . . . Probably the person wouldn't have bothered to read through the whole folder. They only had to weigh it, and they knew what to expect. I'd look my new head teacher in the eye and I'd know I was labelled: *doomed*.

This time it was worse, because I had thought we were settled. I'd lived down my bad name. I was starting to fit in.

'You mean, you think your mother is planning to do another bunk?'

'There are bad signs . . . I wish she'd stop to think what she's doing to my life—'

'I suppose this means your father's traced her again,' said Dita, matter-of-factly.

I winced. We'd talked about my family problems. I'd told her what I knew, or guessed, about the fear that ruled our lives.

I had never known my real father. I didn't know his name. We called ourselves 'Chapman', which was the name of Alan Chapman, Elsa and Max's dad. Mum wouldn't talk about my real dad, not ever. They'd parted, she said, when I was a very young baby, and she hadn't heard from him since. But since Alan died in that car crash, we had been living like people on the run. I could remember dimly that it had been the same before Mum and Alan met, when it was Mum and me on our own. We'd never stayed in one place long. I didn't *know* anything, not for sure. Mum didn't talk and I didn't ask. But by the time I'd grown out of thinking the police might come and take Beano away, and lock us up for being foreign, I had started to suspect what the real problem might be. I'd seen all the signs in the way she behaved. We were on the run. And if we weren't in danger from *the authorities*, it didn't take much imagination to work out who the enemy might be.

Though I'd confided in Dita, I didn't like having the problem spelled out like that. 'I don't *know*,' I said cautiously. She always liked to leap straight to the point, much too fast for me. 'I've told you, I don't *know* anything. I can't prove it. I don't actually *know* if my real father's alive or dead. But something's wrong, and it's the same thing, if you see what I mean. Same as the other times. She thinks someone's after us, spying on us. Except, it's different . . . She went out one evening last week. She was supposed to be going to the Community Fun Day planning meeting. But I don't think she did, because I asked her about it, and she looked completely blank. That's something new. Not part of the pattern—'

Dita grinned. 'Whoa. Adult woman goes out on her own. Weird. Come off it, Andrei. That doesn't sound too bad.'

'You don't understand. My mother *does not go out*. And I've seen her talking to people on the High Street – strangers. Mum doesn't talk to people!'

'Do you think it could have been your father?'

'I don't think so. It was different people. One was a woman.'

'Could have been in deep disguise—'

'Don't laugh. This is serious.'

Dita was wolfing her pancake and chips as if she was starving. I suppose she must have been, after three days. She pushed back her hair. It was growing out an inch of glossy black at the roots, from when she'd bleached it and dyed it red at Christmas. 'If you want some chips,' she advised, 'you'd better be quick. Look, Andrei, I don't want to lose you. You're the best friend I've got. The situation doesn't sound too drastic to me. I hope you're imagining things. But no matter what, isn't it time you talked to her? I mean, about your father? It's crazy, the way you never ask her any questions. Families don't work like that.'

Mine did. Hers didn't. You'd think, from the way Dita behaved, that her family would be unconventional too. In their own way they were very traditional, family-values sort of people. Her mother was an accountant and her father was a doctor. They were totally different from Mum and me, socially speaking, but they respected Dita, and they accepted me as her choice of friend. They'd been very kind to me. They regularly invited me to Sunday lunch at their house, which was their weekly family gathering: Dita and her parents and her grandmother and her married brother and his wife and their children – all round a big table with fancy cutlery and a linen tablecloth. All of them talking fit to bust, arguing and gossiping and asking each other awkward questions. Dita and her brother had furious rows, and her parents joined in, and her gran and her sister-in-law, while I sat there amazed, *keeping my head down*. I couldn't believe the risks that these people took. To me family life had always been like thin ice: terribly thin ice, that I crept over step by step, trying not to think of the terror lurking under the surface.

Dita's mother had told me that all Hindu names are from Sanskrit, their ancient holy language. Her own name was Pushpa, which means a flower. Dita was called Mudita, which means joy and delight. Once she'd asked me what my mother's family name was, originally. She was curious, but not in any nasty way. She thought it was interesting to know about where people come from, and about different cultures. I told her – Milada Nihilo. Dita's mum looked at me strangely and said: '*Nihilo* means "nothing", Andrei. It's a Latin word.'

I looked at Dita across the café table. I thought of those big, happy, noisy Sunday lunches, and I felt helpless. My mother called herself by a name that meant nothing. We lived in fear of someone unseen, who might be my father. It wasn't just Mum who wanted to keep her secrets; it was me, too. There were questions I would never ask. I didn't want the ice to break. But how could I expect Dita to understand?

'I can't ask her. She'd get upset. And she'd be even more determined to run.'

'All right. Maybe you should – well, tell someone else about your mum. There's such a thing as counselling.'

'No! Mum would *hate* that. So would I. We can cope. We've always coped.'

I knew Mum would be horrified at the idea of counselling. We never even saw an ordinary doctor or a dentist, unless it was some kind of examination or injection they sneaked up on you at school. Mum wouldn't have anything to do with them.

Dita frowned at me impatiently. 'But this is no good. You can't go on running all your life. If your father is really following you around the country, it's time you found out for certain. It would be for the best. You and your mum could face him together, and then you'd be free. You wouldn't have to be afraid any more.'

'I'm not *afraid*,' I protested.

Dita shrugged. 'All right, maybe you're not. But your mum certainly is, from what you've told me; and it's making your life a misery.'

I was beginning to wish I'd never raised the subject. I'd only wanted a bit of sympathy. Unfortunately, Dita was the sort of person who couldn't see a problem without jumping in and trying to *do something*. I backtracked as best I could. 'Look, the fact is, Mum's been in a bad way since Dad died. She's been convinced that there's someone following us around, and she's moved us fifteen times a year, it feels like, to get away from this person. I've never seen him; I don't know if "he" really exists. Maybe it's just Mum's imagination, her bad nerves. I've been worried this week because a couple of strange things have happened. But generally, she's getting better. She's been almost normal again since we moved here . . . Meanwhile, my "real father" is probably alive and well and living in – um – in Walsall, with a wife and two kids, a fat labrador and a Vauxhall Astra . . . and never gives a thought to his long-lost former family.'

I looked around Agnelli's: the D-shaped tables with their chipped yellow tops, the metal chutney bowls, the poor-taste salt and pepper shakers shaped like jolly red and orange fruit, the wall behind the counter, covered in ancient posters for Hindu movies and multiethnic local bands, some of them dating back to 1991. I knew the whole dog-eared array by heart. There was a Bhangra compilation playing, the same tape I'd been hearing in here for months. It was so blessedly ordinary and familiar, I could have cried.

'I don't want to delve into my mum's past,' I complained, trying to laugh. 'I just want to be normal – to live in one place, have a routine sort of life. That's all I ask.'

The attempted laugh wasn't a big success. Dita looked at me, her big eyes full of kindness. She reached over and squeezed my hand. 'Don't worry, Andrei,' she said. 'I'll sort your parent problem for you. I'll think of something.'

Then I did laugh. 'You'll think of something! Like the time you blew up Mr Carter's poor old Mazda to save the planet? Oh, great. Now I'm *definitely* worried.'

The net result of this conversation with Dita was not good. I had lied to her, but I couldn't lie to myself; I was afraid. I could try to pretend he didn't exist, that he was a figment of my mother's imagination, the man who followed us around. It made no difference. If our enemy had found us again, I knew what would happen next. He wouldn't come and knock on the door. He wouldn't call us on the telephone. But he would be hanging about on corners as we went by; and Mum would see him, though we wouldn't. He would let Mum know, somehow, where he was living – and there'd be a house or a street, or a block of flats that would fill her with fascinated terror. He would trail us round the stacks in the supermarket. He would wait across the road at the school gates. When we took Max to the playground on the Common he would be staring from a distance . . .

I didn't know what he looked like. I'd never seen a photograph. There'd never been any evidence of his existence, except for my Mum's terror. For all the *proof* I had, what I'd told Dita could be true. But the fear was real. It had poisoned my life. And I knew that once the fear began, it would only get worse until we packed our bags and fled.

Dita was right. We couldn't run and hide forever. I was getting too old to accept the kind of life we had. I wanted to fight back. But maybe, like Mum, I'd been afraid too long. I couldn't get rid of the feeling that if I found out the whole truth it would be *worse*: something worse than I could possibly imagine.

I watched Mum like a hawk. I didn't spot anything suspicious – no unusual phone calls, no strange newspapers with circled items in the Situations Vacant columns. That didn't mean much. She could be very secretive. There was no doubt that her calm phase had ended. She had that all-too-familiar look of panic around her eyes. She'd started getting irritable and snapping at Max and Elsa and me. Or else she'd sit brooding and silent, her mouth pinched and her eyes wide and dark, staring at nothing.

About two weeks after I'd talked to Dita, I came home from school and Mum asked me to take the kids to the library. It was almost Spring. The buds on the city trees were swelling. Some had a froth of greeny-yellow tree-type flowers. We walked along in the bright daylight, the surprising afternoon daylight of early March. I was pushing the buggy and Elsa was alongside, hauling a plastic carrier full of picture books. She wanted to hang it on the buggy's handles, but I was in a bad mood and wouldn't let her. I was in a bad mood because I was sure I'd caught Mum talking about a new job in another town. The way she'd dropped the phone as if it had bitten her, the moment I walked in the door, was very suspicious. I was thinking about people who lived in the same house all their lives. People who had cars and personal computers and video games consoles and new clothes. I was thinking about Dita. You can believe I was not very good company.

I would have liked to be more than friends with Dita Mukarjee. Sometimes I thought she felt the same about me. I couldn't do anything about it. I could have her as a friend. I couldn't have a *girlfriend* who was wild and reckless. I owed it to Mum and Max and Elsa to be sensible. Dita was committed to her craziness and her schemes to save the world. It would never work . . . She had given me a present at Christmas. It was a little black stone statue of Ganesh, the Elephant. He's the Hindu god who's in charge of knowledge and teaching, but he is also called the Lord of Beginnings. He watches over the start of anything new. Dita had told me that, and she said I should keep him in my pocket as a luck charm. I understood what she meant. But there was no point in us beginning anything. I'd be gone in a month or so.

The day before, I had met my mother out on the street by the Monument. I was coming home from school. She was with Max in his buggy, standing outside the Egyptian Food Store with two other people. The three of them were together, but pretending not to be together, like secret agents. There was my mum, and a little fat black woman all wrapped up in a jumble of coats and shawls – almost a bag-lady – and a tall, thin white man in a sharp, dark suit. It looked so strange. I didn't quite know why, but I'd waited 'til she walked away from them to go up to her. She said she'd been taking Elsa round to have tea with a friend from school. I asked her who she'd been talking to. I was sure for a moment that she was going say she hadn't been talking to anyone, but she changed her mind.

'Some people I have to do business with,' she told me.

I asked her if it was about the Community Fun Day, because I couldn't think what other 'business' my mother would have. She said, *Yes, in a way.* I knew she was lying, and she looked so afraid. What was going on? Did we have one enemy or many? Or was it really, after all, just in her mind? Maybe Dita was right and she needed help . . . I'd coped with Mum's weird ways for years, but suddenly I had no strength left. I couldn't go on like this.

Elsa broke in on my gloomy thoughts. 'Andrei, we have to cross the road here.'

I woke up and looked around. 'No we don't. It's quicker to go straight on.'

'But we *can't.*'

I couldn't figure out what she was talking about. Then I realised. Since Elsa set up her famous spell of protection, she and Max had acted as if they were *physically incapable* of stepping outside the magic circle. Elsa had worked on Max. If he was in the buggy and you tried to pushed it through, he'd howl. It shows you what kind of life my family was leading. The fact that the kids refused to go a step beyond their little familiar circuit didn't matter. Our whole existence was in this tiny patch of streets. If I'd been in a better mood, I'd have done what she wanted. After all, we'd had no more pieces of litter trying to cat-burgle us since she did her spell. Today I hated that stupid map. If Mum hadn't found out what Elsa was doing, maybe she'd have forgotten about the empty house.

'Sorry. I'm in a hurry. I have homework to do this evening.'

I gritted my teeth and forged on. Max started to yell. I ignored him. It gave me some satisfaction, at least. I didn't look to see if Elsa was coming. I didn't look round for her until we reached the High Street. I'd have been in trouble if she'd gone off by herself. But she was there beside me. I grabbed her arm without speaking, and marched them over the pedestrian crossing. Once we reached the library, we would be back in the ring. I will admit, I quickened my pace somewhat as we hit the last block before that haven. If you spend a lot of time with little kids, their games start to seem as important as anything in the real world. I stopped at the doors feeling triumphant, cheered up by my fearless act of defiance.

'There,' I grinned. 'You see. Nothing terrible happened.'

Max had given up crying. Elsa, surprisingly, was not angry. She stared at me, almost with admiration. 'Not yet.'

'What d'you mean? We're back inside your circle now.'

She shook her head. 'You broke the spell. I don't know if I can mend it. I certainly can't mend it now. We have no protection, and we're a long way from home.'

—— 32 ——

'Oh well,' I said, trying not to laugh, 'let's hope the ghost wasn't looking at his security monitors.'

When we came out of the library it had started to rain. I bundled them into their waterproofs and we headed back. I followed the proper route this time, turning right down the High Street, towards the Common. I thought I might as well. I walked fast. I told myself it was because I didn't like getting wet. The familiar shops chugged by: *Occasions*, the card shop where Max liked to stop so he could look at the little teddy bears in the window display: the organic butchers, where we bought real meat once in a blue moon, the Cancer Research Campaign shop, where we bought our stylish clothes; Chunky the Bakers, where we bought our iced buns if we could afford a treat; the midget supermarket where we did our main food shopping, McDonalds, where Elsa's schoolmates had their birthday parties . . .

I was never embarrassed about pushing Max's buggy. I'd done it too often. It was a hell of a lot easier than getting him to walk. In fact, Mum and I planned to keep on pushing him around until he was about eight. So I was puzzled, when I noticed how uncomfortable I was feeling. It was as if everybody was looking at me. They pretended not to be, but I knew they were turning to stare after we'd gone by, and whispering to one another. We passed two old ladies outside the launderette. I glanced around furtively. The two ladies were having a good gossip. Behind them someone quickly dodged out of sight – but not quite quickly enough. I was not imagining things. There was someone following us.

I didn't think of Elsa's anti-ghost spell, not then. I thought of my mum. It had always been Mum who could see him; I'd never had so much as a single glimpse . . . I felt a shock, as if I'd passed through an invisible barrier. Something had changed! Maybe it was because I was older and more alert. Maybe the enemy was getting careless. I didn't care which. With the shock came a surge of anger. I thought of the sly torture Mum had endured, on other streets in other towns, through the years . . . Well, I wasn't going to put up with it. I wasn't going to be tormented. I'd catch him in the act.

I stopped and peered into a shop window. I could see our reflections, hanging faintly among the washing machines and fridges of Hanran's DSS Approved Recon Centre (where we'd bought our consumer durables). Me with my black curly hair and pale brown complexion, Elsa with her sleek, fair bob and grey eyes, Max's tufty blond head and bulldog jowls. They took after their father, Max more than Elsa – poor kid. He was a lovely man, but no one could have called Alan good-looking. That wasn't what I was stopping for. I wanted a better look at whoever was following us. And there he was. I caught him, the figure on the edge of sight: the fear man. I felt a spurt of adrenalin, almost like joy. *At last.* Something I could get hold of! The next instant, I knew he'd spotted my trick because he vanished from the reflected street. I barely stopped to stamp on the brake of the buggy before I ran, back up the rainy pavement, dodging late shoppers and their umbrellas. There were no side streets near; he couldn't get away. I'm a fast runner; I knew I could catch him.

He was thin, and wearing a long, grey coat; he had a grey hat pulled down over his eyes. He was hurrying with his head down, trying to look inconspicuous. I saw him dodge into the loading bay by the side of the supermarket, a place where our local down-and outs liked to shelter. I grinned as I ran. I knew I had him. I swung in there. It was a lightless concrete bunker that ended in blank, high doors. The grey man was up against the wall with his back to me, as if he was trying to push his way through. I caught a whiff of old decay, like a fog lying over the usual stink of pee and stale wine and exhaust fumes.

'Hey, you!' I yelled. He turned and looked at me. I saw

an empty clown's face: black eyes, black nostrils, black, gaping mouth.

But I'd caught him, and I didn't care. I grabbed him by the arm.

'What's the matter with you?' I snarled. 'What do you want from us?'

The sleeve I was holding was matted with dirt. The man peered bleerily through a fuzz of face-hair and breathed horrible fumes at me. I'd nabbed old Carlsberg Special, one of the loading bay's regulars. He was a peaceable character, with his rotting camel-hair coat and his wire trolley of possessions, and his toothless smile. I knew him well. I'd seen him hundreds of times, shambling around his little beat.

'Nuffin',' he garbled, looking terrified. 'Nuffin' guv. Nuffin', sir. Honest.'

'Sorry,' I said. 'I thought you were someone else.'

'I wish I was,' mumbled old Carlsberg. 'No such luck.'

But the grey man, the fear man, had vanished.

Max and Elsa were where I had left them, alone on the pavement by the Recon Centre. They stared at me. Max was in his blue all-over suit, that he was growing out of at the wrists and ankles; Elsa in her yellow cagoule. In the pointed hoods of their rain gear, they looked like two sinister little gnomes.

'I'm sorry,' I explained, lamely. 'I thought I saw someone.'

I found I was clutching Ganesh in my jacket pocket. If ever I'd needed a lucky charm, this was the time. Elsa had a peculiar expression – scared and yet triumphant.

'I told you so,' she said.

That evening, Mum was going out on Fun Day business. I was babysitting. She'd told me she was going out for a drink with someone called Celie. They were going to talk about the 'attraction' that had been assigned to Mum. She'd volunteered to run the Hall of Mirrors, apparently: a kind of magic show. I knew who Celie was. She had a daughter of fifteen who went to our school, and a boy in the juniors at Elsa's school . . . But I wasn't sure if I believed in this meeting. I *knew* Mum had lied to me about going to the other one.

I was very puzzled altogether by this 'Fun Day' development. I'd never known my mother to get involved with strangers or make friends with anyone at all. I watched her getting ready. She was looking nice. She was wearing her shawl with the blue spangles that I remembered from long ago. But to me the whole thing seemed false.

I couldn't resist asking, 'There's nothing else? You're *really* going out with Celie?'

She was arranging the shawl around her shoulders, looking at herself in the mirror over the living room's defunct fireplace, which now held a big glass jar of dry grasses and stuff. I thought she would snap at me, but she didn't.

'Is there any reason why not?'

I couldn't work it out. I knew she was scared, as scared as she'd ever been before. I'd seen her face when she spoke of the house in Roman Road. I'd seen her moods over the last few weeks. And today, for the first time in my life, I had spotted the fear man myself (though he'd got away somehow, and left me grabbing at shadows in the supermarket loading bay). All the signs were there. Yet I hadn't caught her making any preparations to run away.

'You're not planning another getaway?'

'No, Andrei. Not this time.'

'Okay,' I said. 'I believe you. It's hard to adjust, that's all.'

Her eyes met mine in the mirror. 'Did you always mind moving, so much?'

'Yes.'

'You never said so.'

'I didn't think I had a choice. You've been like God to me, or the weather. Today it's going to rain, today it's going to be sunny, today we're going to move house. I didn't know I could do anything about it.'

'Hmm. But now you're growing up. Things have to change, I know that. And things will change.' She looked very serious suddenly, as if she was making a promise. Then she smiled. 'Lock up carefully behind me. I won't be late.'

As soon as I'd bolted and locked up behind Mum, Elsa came downstairs in her pink woolly dressing-gown. She walked past me, took her drawing book and a pencil case from the table and settled herself, firmly, on the rug in front of the television.

'Get back to bed.'

She didn't even look round.

'Do you really think something's going to happen? Don't be stupid.'

No response. So we sat for a while, both of us not-watching the tv. It went on talking to itself quietly, about coral reefs being destroyed by global warming off the coast of Australia. I'd decided to abandon my homework. I didn't think I could concentrate.

It's strange, how memory works. I wasn't paying any attention at the time, but I can close my eyes now and see the pictures that were on the screen that evening: the coloured fish, the coral, some frothy purple seaweed. For ages, it seemed, nothing happened. I knew that Elsa believed the ghost was coming to get us, because I'd broken her spell of protection. Images of the fear man, the grey man with the empty clown face, kept floating into my head. But I wasn't afraid, not really afraid. I didn't know *what* to believe.

I counted over the positive things. Mum had gone out to meet a friend, like a normal person. Better than that: she'd actually admitted that I had some human rights in this household, at last. This was good going. All right, I was pretty sure someone had been following us in the High Street. I'd chased him down the street until he'd managed to get away. But there was no ghost. The ghost was an old newspaper flapping against the garden fence; a bundle of rubbish drifting in the wind. It was a rat or a mouse or something, moving the litter on the doormat of the empty house. In a moment I'd send Elsa off to bed, and I would stop thinking idiotic thoughts.

There was a wind rising. It rattled round our house, making pattering, rustling noises in the street outside. It's going to rain again, I thought. Mum will get drenched. I stood up. The noise of the wind made me feel I ought to check things, make sure everything was secure. I went to look over Elsa's shoulder. She had collected all the anti-ghost maps, and was methodically rubbing out the jagged 'X's on each one. This upset me. It was silly, but it did.

'Why are you doing that?' I demanded. 'I only broke one.'

'Doesn't matter. You broke the circuit. It's broken.'

'I thought you were going to fix it.' I used my good-brother voice, as if I was kindly joining in her game, which of course didn't mean anything to me. 'Can't you do that?'

Elsa glanced up with a small, grim smile. She wasn't fooled. 'No.'

'I don't think Mum locked the windows,' I said. 'I'd better check.'

The house's owners had had the two downstairs rooms knocked into one. The dining-nook, with the table where we ate and worked and whatever, was at the back by the kitchen door. In the front, facing the street, there were two windows. We had heavy floor-length curtains for them. We'd bought them second-hand and they were shabby but I liked them. They were an orangey-rust colour, like fallen leaves. I pulled them back and checked that the security bolts were in place – which they were, of course. It was about quarter to ten on a windy March night. It wasn't raining, not yet. The street was empty. Parked cars stood along the kerb, staring silently with their big, lidless eyes. The sky above the houses was a fuzzy, pinkish grey. Every streetlight had a damp halo. I could hear the wind, but it looked as if nothing was stirring. There was no sign of the thin grey figure I'd been afraid I'd see.

'There's no one there,' I announced in relief, forgetting that I was just supposed to be checking the locks.

I stayed where I was, staring. I remembered suddenly how fine and magical it had been to walk under the stars with my mother. I was angry because something precious had been polluted. The night used to be *mine*, mine and my mother's, our private place . . . Elsa popped up beside me, breaking my train of thought.

'It seems as if we're going to get away with it,' I told her. 'Your ghost has decided to let me off.'

'*Andrei!*' she whispered. '*Look!*'

I had been staring down the street, but the ghost was already here. Where a moment before there'd been nothing, I saw a face pressed against the lower pane of the left-hand window. It was soft and blurred. It had no solid features, only those ragged holes. As we watched, it rose, to the height of a man. It must have been crawling, down on the ground, when I first looked out. Boneless grey hands fumbled on the glass.

I yanked the curtains shut and backed away from them.

'Get to bed, Elsa. Get in your room and shut the door.'

'You must be *kidding!*' breathed my little sister.

At least she'd seen it too. At least I wasn't going crazy. But I didn't know what to do.

'Do you think it's still there?' I whispered after a moment.

'Let's look.'

It was crazily brave, but I felt the same way. We had to look. I opened the curtain a crack, terrified that I might find myself staring right into that face. It wasn't there. I pulled the folds of heavy cloth wide. No sign of the ghost. 'It's gone!' I laughed aloud. 'Well, thank goodness for that. I don't know what it was, some kind of optical illusion, reflection. Maybe some joker in a Hallowe'en mask, someone trying to scare us . . .'

My voice trailed away. Every muscle of my body went rigid. *Because it was there, not three metres away from me.* It was standing beside the street light in front of our house, the skeleton-thin body almost invisible against the light. It seemed to be looking up, as if it was deciding how to break in. Behind me the tv went on talking, calmly, about tropical reefs.

'I'm going out.'

If that sounds completely insane, all I can say is you had to be there. I didn't disbelieve my eyes, I didn't disbelieve the way I felt, but I had to know. If there was a ghost out there I had to touch it, prove it. Elsa followed me into the hall. Our front door was actually two doors, with a kind of air-lock between them that held a doormat and a row of coathooks. It was awkward, but Mum liked the arrangement. She said it made the house easier to heat. I knew that she felt safer with two doors she could lock. I didn't switch on the light. I didn't want to alert whatever it was – though I don't know what difference light or dark could make to a ghost.

'Don't!' whispered Elsa frantically. '*Don't.* Don't you see, it wants you out there. It's been sent to get us. Don't do what it wants. Andrei – *Don't!*'

I didn't take any notice. I was wrestling with the bolt on the inner door. It was stuck.

'Stop it!' she wailed. 'Get back! Get away from there—'

Suddenly she grabbed for the light switch. Our front hall leapt into yellow brilliance. I was furious because she'd given the thing warning. But a tiny rustling sound made me look at the door in front of me. There was something moving. There was a grey thing, like a thin grey caterpillar, wriggling along the crack above the lock, between the inner door and its frame. I leapt backwards – at least, I don't remember doing it but I must have. Next moment I was at the bottom of the stairs, clutching on to Elsa.

We crouched there, staring. I could hear her breathing, I could feel the beat of her heart. I thought of Max upstairs in his cot. I had to get them out of this. But I couldn't move, I couldn't do anything. Gradually, the grey caterpillar oozed its way in. It became a paper-thin hand, that groped over the panels of the door. The hand was followed, horribly slowly, by an arm, and then the creature's side, and then one leg; and it went on coming. The head came in last, tugging its way through the knife-blade gap with a minute popping sound. It stood in our hall. The clown-face looked at us, the two dark dents of its eyes empty and dead. A smell of dirt and decay wafted towards us.

Then something happened to me. The thing made my hair stand on end, and terrified me so much I could have wet myself. I couldn't bear to be so frightened. And somewhere in me, I think I'd grasped that it could do no more. Fear was all the power it possessed. I yelled. I leapt at the ghost and grabbed it. Something horribly soft seemed to move, to squirm in my grip, trying to escape. I didn't let go. I held on with one hand, and swung a punch at its face. But my punch went right *through* the face. I gasped and yelled again. It was such a sickening, weird kind of relief to find that it could be touched, that I could damage it. After that I went mad for a minute. I punched the blank face again and again. I hauled on its arm until one long rip detached half its body from its neck and down through the trunk. The head fell to the floor and I kicked it to pulp. I hauled its arms out of their sockets, snapped its legs at the knees, dragged hanks of entrails from its belly . . . I tore that monster limb from limb!

Then the ghost was in a heap on the floor. But it had

changed. It wasn't a ghost any more. It was a messy, dirty pile of rubbish: old newspaper, grit, grease, cat hairs, scraps of food cartons. I stood blinking at it, feeling dizzy and bewildered. How did *that* happen . . . ? In a daze, I opened the inner door and the front door, and started clearing the mess outside. I carried the ghost, handful by handful, and dropped it in the gutter. I remember thinking: *I hope no one spots me doing this. It's anti-social, dumping litter on the street.* But the wind would soon blow it away. When I'd cleared out every scrap, I staggered back towards the house. I was carrying a piece of its arm as a trophy. I was grinning all over my face, the kind of mad too-wide grin that makes your jaws ache. Elsa stood in the doorway.

'There you are, Elsa.' I waved the rag of arm at her. 'I sure taught that monster a lesson! I don't know how it got through the door the way it did. Must have been a freak gust of wind that pushed it through the crack. But there you are,' I repeated. My teeth were chattering with shock and relief. 'No ghost. Merely another freak litter-incident!'

For a moment, I think I believed that.

'Andrei!' She was staring past me.

I looked back. I saw the grey shreds move. The wind was trying to carry them off, but they crawled towards each other. We watched as the ghost remade itself. When it was done it came towards us, flopping and waving and bending double as the wind played with it. It reached out its boneless, broken arms. The ragged slit of a mouth opened and moved.

'Give it back!' hissed Elsa. '*Give it back! Give it back!*'

I realised what she meant and threw my trophy, desperately. I didn't think it would do any good. I was sure the ghost would still come on. It didn't. The fragment was taken up, somehow. The figure seemed to turn away from us. Then it was nothing again: an old newspaper, blowing off down the road. We went inside. I locked the doors. I wondered what my face looked like. It felt as if it was fixed in permanent lines of eye-popping terror. I'd have to have plastic surgery. I noticed that the smell was clinging to me, and my hands were filthy.

'I'm going to bed,' announced Elsa, in a strange, strained little voice. 'You'd better wash your hands and face before Mum comes home. You look awful.'

She sounded as if she was in shock or something, but I let her go. I didn't know what else to do. I did more than wash my face. I had a shower, and put everything I'd been wearing in the washing machine. When I'd done that I looked in on the kids. Max was fast asleep, so was Elsa. I went down and sat listening to the washing machine as it thumped and churned. I kept trying to think about what had happened, to make sense of it. My brain felt like a gearwheel trying to catch and failing, over and over again. I had fought with the ghost and won. Fought with the ghost, the shadow that followed us, the fear man . . .

No, not with the fear man himself. I remembered what Elsa had screamed at me when I was trying to open the door. *It's been sent to get us!* I felt she was right, if anything about this crazy horror made sense. The thing I'd fought wasn't a person, dead or alive. It was a puppet, a shadow, a messenger. But the fear man had sent it.

How could my father be the master of a ghost?

Who was he? What was he?

That night, I fell asleep the moment I lay down, and had some choice dreams, I can tell you. Next night I didn't sleep at all. I didn't mind. I was better off awake. I lay there thinking for hours. Mum hadn't made any comment when she came back and found me doing a load of washing at ten past eleven. And of course I'd said nothing about the ghost. She had her secrets, I had mine . . . There'd always been things I didn't tell Mum. It's not natural to tell your parents everything. But we couldn't go on like this. Dita was right; of course Dita was right. I had to start asking those questions.

Next morning it was the normal weekday bustle. I'd made the tea and carried it from the kitchen to the dining nook (our kitchen is too small for anyone to eat in it). I was making toast. Mum was putting out cereal and milk for Max. He was sitting at his baby-table beside the big one, singing something about stay-dry nappies that he'd picked up from the tv. Elsa had filled her own cereal bowl and was eating it the way she likes it – dry, with no sugar – on the rug in front of the early morning cartoons. I buttered my toast and brought it in, with a piece for Mum – which she would nibble and then abandon, as usual – and her veggie juice. I had geared myself up to say, *Mum, we have to talk. Can we have a serious talk tonight?*

It didn't come out like that.

'Mum, is my father alive or dead?'

I was horrified at myself, and terrified at what she might answer. I hoped she hadn't heard me, that I'd been drowned out by the nappy song. But she'd heard.

She drained her glass. 'He's alive,' she said dryly.

We had not discussed this person, not ever. It would have been more natural if she'd said: *Why do you suddenly ask me that?* Even more natural if she'd said: *For heaven's sake, is this the moment, Andrei? Can't it wait?* Or ignored me completely. I was astonished that she'd answered. I felt as if the world was turning upside-down. Well, at least if he was alive, he couldn't be a ghost. Maybe the thing that came from the empty house, the thing I'd fought, was nothing to do with my father. I had to find out. I stumbled for the right words.

'Is there – was there anything *strange* about him?'

Mum looked into the bottom of her glass. I saw her mouth twist in a wry, crooked smile, as if I'd made a joke about something that wasn't very funny. 'Not really. In his own particular way, your father is a very normal man.'

She looked up, still smiling, as if she was bracing herself to answer whatever I'd ask next. But I was like someone who'd jumped into deep water, forgetting to learn how to swim first. I couldn't think how to go on.

'Oh,' I said, feeling like an idiot. 'I'm glad. Thanks. Thanks for telling me.'

Mum sighed. She stood up, pushing her chair back. 'Elsa, have you finished? Come here, and let me brush your hair. Andrei, have you packed your bag? We're late.'

And that was the end of the discussion.

After school that day, I caught up with Dita as we were all pouring through the gates. We'd been doing different classes; it was the first time I'd managed to get near her. She was with a posse of girls; they were all going off somewhere together. We were friends, not boyfriend/girlfriend, and I didn't like to lay claim to her company as if I had special rights. Usually, if she was doing something with other people, I said hi and left them to it, and she did the same with me. But this time, I insisted. So she knew it was important.

We went to Agnelli's. The place was full; we were lucky to get a table to ourselves.

'You look awful, Andrei,' she told me. 'What's the matter?'

'I'm all right.'

'You don't look it. Is it your mother? Is she going to make you leave school?'

'No . . . I mean, I don't know. It isn't about that. At least, maybe it isn't.'

I'd been trying to decide exactly what to tell her. I couldn't bring myself to describe what had happened the night before last. But I had a plan.

'Do you believe in ghosts?'

'Yes,' she answered, as if it was the most natural thing. Trust Dita.

'Real ghosts?' I probed. 'The spirits of dead people walking around? Things you can p-put your hand through?' I swallowed hard. 'But they keep on coming?' I drank some of my coffee, trying not to meet her eyes. I knew my voice was shaking.

'Well,' she said slowly, 'I don't know what ghosts are. They could be the spirits of dead people. Or they could be some kind of trick in time, so that you see an impression of something that happened in the past. Or something else entirely. I've never seen a ghost myself, or heard or felt one. But I do believe in them, yes. I believe people see apparitions, of some kind, in certain places. The *place* usually seems to be important. What about you?'

'What? Me?' I knew I sounded guilty and nervous, I couldn't help it.

'Have you ever seen a ghost?'

'I don't know.' I tried to drink more coffee, but the cup was empty. 'I'm not sure. Dita, how would you like to help me break into a haunted house?'

She stared. Without answering, she picked up my cup. 'I'll get you another coffee. Double sugar, isn't it?' She raised her eyebrows. 'I'd better make it treble sugar.'

She came back with the coffee. I drank it very hot, and Agnelli's took on a more solid appearance. Dita grinned. 'Good, you look slightly more lifelike. I thought you were going to faint on me, for a moment. So tell me about the haunted house. I'm with you. But I'm not keen on breaking in anywhere—'

'It's not going to be a burglary. The house is empty. We're simply going to get ourselves inside, discreetly, and have a look around.'

So I told her about the house on Roman Road: how we'd

come across the place one day, and Elsa and I had started to investigate, and Elsa claimed she'd seen a ghost.

'But did *you* see it?'

'I'm not sure,' I muttered again.

And I *wasn't* sure. In daylight everything looks different. Real and unreal change around. Things that seemed certain in the night fade away and disappear. It's as if there are two worlds and one is stronger than the other.

Her eyes narrowed. 'What does this have to do with your parent problem?'

'I don't know,' I said. 'It might not be connected at all. But . . . it might be.'

I rubbed my hands over my eyes, which felt buggy and boiled with tiredness. I had tried to talk to my mother, and failed. I couldn't try again. There was one other option. I had to go back to the house on Roman Road. Whatever was happening, that place was somehow the focus. We would go there, Dita and I, and find out the truth.

I hoped, and I tried to believe, that we'd find a rational explanation for everything.

'You see, strange things have been happening. You know how my mother behaves as if she's on the run; and I've thought it might be because my father was following us around. This is . . . well, it's different, but . . .' I did not want to go into details. 'But I think someone may be squatting in that empty house and using it as a base while he tries to spook us, to frighten us; not just Mum but me and the kids as well this time –'

'Your father!'

It was a statement, not a question. I half nodded. 'Well, yes. Could be. I'd tell you more, but I don't want to . . . to prejudice you, I think that's the word. I want you to go into the house and see whatever you see without any cues from me.'

'You mean, you *have* seen something?'

'No. I mean, I'm not going to tell you anything more.'

Dita's black eyes snapped with sudden temper. 'In other words, you don't trust me. You want me to be your miner's canary. If I scream, the ghost is real? But I'm crazy, remember? Loopy Dita Mukarjee. What would it prove if I started seeing things?'

She didn't raise her voice, not much. But she'd hit a moment of comparative hush in Agnelli's babble. Heads turned all over the café.

'You don't have to shout.' I could understand why she was annoyed. But it was because I trusted her, more than I trusted myself, that I didn't want to say more. 'Please. I *will* explain, honestly. Only you have to come to the house first.'

She was still glowering. 'Oh, all right. But this haunt had better be good.'

The Mukarjees lived a short bus ride away, in the nice streets with trees in them in them on the other side of the Common. I walked with Dita to the Monument. She teased me most of the way, to make me tell her more. I wouldn't. The cherry trees in the War Memorial plot were in bloom behind their railings. Dita jumped on to her bus, laughing, with cherry blossom petals in her hair. I was left alone on the familiar street where I'd begun to feel at home. It had turned hostile and mysterious. I looked for Mum's strange friends. I didn't see them, but I could feel them watching me.

Three

*T*HAT SATURDAY, EVERYONE INVOLVED IN THE FUN DAY was supposed to come to our local Community Centre. They were going to review the stock – sort out the tents and the ropes and the parade costumes, and see what needed to be fixed or replaced. It was an annual event, kind of a social as well as a working party; it would last the whole day. I knew Mum had decided to go along with Elsa and Max. Dita's mother would be there too. She was a Fun Day regular. I'd arranged to meet Dita there. It seemed like a good opportunity to slip away, leaving Mum and the children safely occupied. (I'd had to accept, by this stage, that my mum's involvement in the Fun Day was genuine, though I still couldn't understand it.)

Actually, the stock review looked like fun. I had never been inside the Community Centre before. I'd never been involved in anything like this. I think I'd have enjoyed it if I hadn't had other things on my mind. The big hall was in chaos. There were battered cartons spilling brightly coloured scraps of costume, there were people holding up tattered garlands and streamers. Fun Day clerical assistants hunched over trestle tables, making reams of lists. There were people crawling over the canvas of a huge tent, as if they'd skinned a giant elephant; people checking through bags full of pegs and ropes; adults and children milling around in all directions. It was intriguing to see faces I knew: Mr and Mrs Mukarjee, Salvatore and Sunny and Sunny's mother; Celie and her kids; Mr Archer, the butcher from the High Street. Though I looked carefully, I didn't see the man or the woman that my mother had been talking to outside the Egyptian shop.

Mrs Mukarjee roped me in to help Dita, who was counting angels' wings.

'It was the Heavens last year,' she explained. 'This year, the parade theme is Oceans. What we will do, is we will sew the wing tips together and they will make seashell head-dresses. With some greeny-blue crêpe streamers, that will look very effective . . .'

'My mother, the cock-eyed optimist,' groaned Dita. 'It'll look terrible. The parade is a disaster, every year. I hate it.' But I knew she didn't mean it. I envied her. I wished I could be part of something so comforting and happy.

Dita and I left at the first tea break. I'd told Mum we had no special plans. We were going to hang out, maybe look at the shops, and I'd be home for tea. We didn't talk. I could tell Dita was still annoyed with me. As we reached the nearest bus stop, something made me turn round. Elsa was coming after us. Dita and I looked at each other. She didn't have a little sister, but she did have nieces. She knew about brats. She groaned.

'I'll handle this,' I said.

Elsa came up and stood there in her shabby red school jacket, worn over her favourite green dress with the full skirt and baggy-kneed purple leggings (my sister has terrible taste in clothes).

'You're going to the haunted house, aren't you,' she declared.

'Get back to the hall,' I told her. 'You're supposed to be with Mum. She'll go crazy if she looks round and you're not there.'

'I told her you and Dita were taking me with you. She doesn't mind. Have some *sense* Andrei. You know you need me.'

I had no idea how she'd guessed where we were going, and I didn't ask.

'You are being a total pest, Elsa. Do as you're told.'

She scowled. Her jaw set obstinately. '*I am coming with you.*'

When Elsa looked like that, *nothing* would make her give in. I'd have to pick her up and carry her back, kicking and screaming, and then what would Mum think?

'Oh, let her come along,' broke in Dita impatiently, while I was hesitating. 'What difference does it make?'

So we took the bus to Roman Road together, Dita and Elsa and I. It was a cold day, but bright. The sky was blue, there were spring flowers in front gardens. It was strange to see the house again. I hadn't known how the place had been looming and growing in my brain. It looked smaller than I'd remembered it. The chunks of dirt that I had dug out of the carved lettering were still lying on the pavement. The tree had produced a few blotchy leaves. There was no-one about. A brown dog trotted by, on its own business. We stood on the pavement, me and Dita dressed for housebreaking in jeans and dark jackets, Elsa in her colourful ensemble. None of us seemed in a hurry to go any further. Dita examined the gateposts.

'*Re* – something.' She tried the other post, picking more gunk from the grooves I hadn't cleared. 'N O C . . . T I S . . . *Noctis*. That's Latin. It means night.'

She looked up at the dead windows and the grime-coated front door. 'The House of Night. Good name for a haunted house. Well, what do we do now?'

2121 Roman Road was on the corner of a side street, so there was a blank wall on one side. On the other there was a boarded-up shop front. It had once been an off-licence. The door was heavily padlocked and there was a metal grille over the boarded window. It looked as if it was in use, but not occupied at present. At least we didn't have to worry about disturbing the neighbours.

'Let's go round the back,' I said.

Behind the houses we found a narrow alleyway between two rows of garden walls. The back entrance to the empty house had a solid wooden gate. It was the same height as the wall on either side, which was about half as tall again as me. It looked decrepit and there was no fastening on the outside, but it didn't shift when I shoved it as hard as I could. I gave Dita a leg up. She sat astride the gate, and held down a hand for Elsa, and then for me. We dropped, one by one, into the garden of the empty house.

The gate was bolted shut on the inside. The bolt and its fittings were one mass of rust, solid and immoveable. We peered out from under the branches of some overgrown evergreen bushes. They had tiny white flowers that gave out a faint, sweet scent. I could see the remains of a garden shed, and a hollow place that might once have been a goldfish pond. There'd been a wooden archway – I think it's called a *pergola* – that had collapsed. The roses that had been trained over it were sprawled across the garden path, in a mass of dead leaves and briars. Beyond that barrier we could see the back door of the house. It was hanging open, crazily aslant in its frame. We could see into a room full of rubble and fallen timbers. I'd brought some tools in a daypack, things I thought might be useful for a burglary. Apparently we weren't going to need them.

Everything was very still, so still it made you feel it was a shame to breathe. It was a sad sort of place, and yet enticing: it invited you to explore. But the sight of the open door seemed to have slowed us down. Nobody stirred for a good minute.

Elsa was the first to break free. 'Come on. We're wasting time.'

Dita stayed where she was. She was rubbing her arms as if she was cold, although the garden was a sheltered spot and it was quite warm.

'Andrei,' she whispered, 'what are you going to do if he's

here? This person who's been scaring you, who might be your father. What if he's at home?'

I shrugged. I had thought about the possibility, but not much. I didn't want to put myself off the idea of breaking in. I was determined to *find out* . . . whatever there was to find.

'I'm not sure that there *is* anybody living in the house. That's one of the things I want to know. If we hear anyone moving, we can run for it, I suppose. If he catches us . . . then I suppose we have a family reunion.'

'And what if it's not your father? What then?'

'You mean, what if it is a real ghost?' I noticed that her voice sounded strange. 'What's the matter, Dita? Are you backing out?' I was surprised at her.

'No,' she said slowly. 'No. But you didn't tell me it would be like this.'

'Like what?'

She stared at me. 'The . . . the atmosphere. You must feel it. You're the one who told me the house was haunted.'

I knew she'd been angry because she thought I was pulling her leg. Now it was my turn to be suspicious. 'I don't feel any different from usual. Are you kidding? Or what?'

'I'm not kidding. I'm *scared.*' She didn't look as if she was joking. She looked surprised and bewildered. 'I know nothing's happened. I just *became scared* the moment I climbed down from that gate. I believe in ghosts, but I didn't know I'd be affected like this—'

'Maybe you're psychic and you never knew it,' I suggested.

She shook her head. 'It isn't funny, Andrei. Whatever it is I feel, it's *frightening.*'

I didn't know what to make of this at all. At least she wasn't annoyed with me any more . . . But Elsa had stopped outside the open door. She was beckoning urgently, so we gave up the discussion and joined her. She pointed to something lying at her feet. It looked like a pink slug, or an amputated tongue. It was slightly different from the others we'd seen. The fleshy colour had a darker tone, and it was flattened at the edges. But it was definitely a ghost egg. I'd forgotten how evil and gross they looked.

Dita crouched next to Elsa and peered, fascinated.

'What is it? It looks like a chicken's heart, but there are no . . . tubes.'

'I've no idea.' (I had *some* idea, but I didn't want to say.) 'But we've found them here before.'

'It's a ghost egg,' Elsa informed her. So much for my plan for Dita to make up her own mind without anyone influencing her. 'Ghosts hatch out of them. I think this one's battery has run down. But don't touch it. Don't even look at it for too long. They're his guard devices.' She stood up. 'We'd better hurry. I did a spell to keep him out of the way – the man who controls the ghosts. He won't know it's a spell, not if it works properly. He'll just think he has to go out, and he'll go. But it won't last for more than a couple of hours.'

Dita stared at her and then at me. 'Your sister *did a spell?*'

'She has hunches.' I tried to make it sound normal. 'She has hunches about things, and calls it "making up spells". I never take much notice.'

Elsa glared at me.

I could see that Dita had started to wonder if we were both crazy. She looked suspicious and disbelieving, and yet still frightened. All she said was, 'Let's get on with it.'

Have you ever investigated a haunted house? It is impossible not to feel two things: excited and stupid. You're bound to feel slightly excited, because an empty house is exciting, and more so if you are deliberately seeking out some kind of spooky experience. You're bound to feel stupid because – well, I ask you. It is a stupid thing to do.

The rubble room had been a kitchen. The ceiling had fallen down. There was a gap overhead, right up to the ceiling of the upstairs room above. We clambered through the mess.

'If someone had moved in here,' remarked Dita, 'they'd have replaced that rust-bucket bolt on the back door, and cleared a path through this lot.'

'Not if they didn't want anyone to know the house was occupied.'

The sink was full of lumps of plaster. Dita tried the taps. Nothing came out except a few flakes of rust. There was nothing else to investigate, unless we started shifting rubble. So we went on. Beyond the kitchen there were three doors on the left, and a dark lobby immediately on our right. At the far end of the passageway I could make out that dank pile of junk mail on the doormat, untouched.

Dita switched on a torch. 'Isn't it *spooky?*' she murmured. 'It feels so *weird.*'

Elsa and I glanced at each other and shrugged. I didn't have to ask. I knew my sister felt the same as I did . . . nothing special.

When we opened the first door on the left we found, unexpectedly, a flight of steps and a passageway leading back under the kitchen. The room at the end was big and square. It must be under the garden. There was a row of little high windows that must look out on that dip in the ground I'd thought was an ex-goldfish pond. A greenish, watery light came down from them. There was no furniture. The floor was filthy, but it seemed to be made of stone, or stone tiles, that showed some glints of colour. When we reached the middle of the room and shone Dita's torch around, we had a surprise. The walls had been decorated with painted pictures – they're called murals – instead of wallpaper. Even by torchlight we could see that there wasn't much left. Damp and age had destroyed the paint. But eyes gleamed out at us, and scraps of gold. In one place there was a bowl of fruit, in another a flowering tree.

'Amazing,' I whispered. 'Treasure!'

Elsa's eyes were shining. 'Maybe it's actual Roman remains. Maybe it was a Roman temple!' There was a niche in one of the walls that looked quite like an altar.

'I doubt it,' I said. 'It's bound to be Victorian reproductions.'

'But it *could* be really old!'

'Excuse me,' muttered Dita. 'It's interesting, but I hate it. I want to get out.'

Elsa and I peered at her in the green gloom, puzzled.

'How exactly *do* you feel?' asked Elsa coolly.

'I feel as if I'm going to be sick,' stated Dita.

It was hard to tell, in the watery light, but she didn't look too healthy.

'It was a good plan to bring someone else here,' Elsa said to me. 'Maybe she can sense a ghost coming. Let's wait and see. If *she* sees something, you finally won't be able to pretend that it's all our imagination.'

I gathered that Elsa and I were both thinking of Dita as a kind of miner's canary. Obviously my sister wasn't scared at all. Neither was I, but I had a feeling I ought to be. I did not want to challenge whatever lived in this house. I didn't want another fight. I only wanted to find out the truth.

'No, I think we ought to listen to our canary. Out of here, before she keels over.'

Dita gave me a shaky grin. We trooped back up to the ground floor.

The second door led to an ordinary, empty room. The third, the front room, was much the same. The floor was bare boards. The young leaves of the tree that grew up outside fluttered against the window panes. There was peeling wallpaper in a pattern of yellow stripes on a dim mauve background. There were pale patches where pictures had been hung, and ragged holes where light fittings had been torn out. On the floor, you could see where the carpet had been laid, and marks where furniture had stood. There was a dried-up dead wasp lying on one of the windowsills, and a lone fir cone in the fire grate. In the alcoves on either side of the fire there were built-in cupboards. They were stone empty.

In the front hall, Dita shone her torch on the pile of junk mail. 'No sign of footprints,' she remarked. There was nothing else of interest either. We went upstairs. There were three bedrooms: one large, one small and one medium; and a bathroom, which was the room with the collapsed floor. The bath, a big old one with claw feet, stood on a surviving raft of planks, looking extremely precarious. There was a tempting little cupboard on the wall above it, but it was out of reach.

They couldn't take the pictures from the sunken room. Everywhere else, someone had stripped this house to the bone. I was watching out for ghost eggs. I was waiting every moment for the foul smell of decay to waft over me; for a grey clown-faced figure to form out of the shadows in an empty corner. Nothing happened. Nothing stirred, not so much as a mouse or a fly. We walked into the biggest bedroom for a closer look. This was the emptiest room yet. There were no cupboards, no closet doors, no shelves, only the walls, floor, and an empty fireplace. It was full of afternoon sunlight. Elsa started to tap the walls, hoping for a hollow sound. Dita switched off her torch.

'Can you tell me what you were expecting to see now? Or is it still a secret?'

I shrugged. 'I didn't know what to expect. I just hoped, like I said and Elsa said, that if something weird happened you'd see it too. So I'd know, once and for all. Elsa has seen things, but that doesn't count. She's always making up stories about ghosts and magic. She doesn't know the difference between fantasy and reality.' I looked at Dita hopefully. 'Do you feel sick in here?'

She glanced around the sunny, empty room. She still had that strange expression. 'Yes, I do. If you don't feel it, I'm sure you think I'm fooling, but it's true. I don't mind telling you, I thought *you* were playing a trick on *me*. You were in a very odd mood when you suggested this expedition. I thought you'd decided to hoax me. And I was annoyed—'

'I wouldn't do that!'

'I didn't think you would, but you *were* behaving strangely. Now I know it's not a hoax. There's something here that affects different people in different ways. You and Elsa have seen ghosts, or think you have; I feel sick.' She frowned, trying to be precise. 'Feeling sick doesn't describe it. This room, the whole house, is full of something that makes me feel – I don't know – like an animal before an earthquake. *I know there's something wrong.* It's a very powerful feeling of *wrongness and danger.* I want to get out of here. I'd run if I was by myself. Do you believe me?'

'I do, but—' I began.

At that moment, there was a heavy thumping noise from somewhere inside the walls. The whole house began to shudder. Elsa yelled, flew across the room and grabbed me. I yelled and grabbed Dita. We clung to each other in blind, shameless panic.

But the juddering and groaning rumbled into silence, and nothing happened.

Dita recovered first. 'I know what *that* was,' she gasped. 'It was the plumbing! Air in the pipes. Remember, I turned the taps on in the kitchen!' She grinned at me. 'Well, now I feel better about my scaredy-cat feelings. You were terrified to death, Andrei.'

'I was not!'

'*Sure* you weren't. But you did have your eyes tight shut.'

'You did!' crowed Elsa. 'I saw them!'

Elsa got the giggles, Dita joined her and so did I. For a couple of minutes we were all laughing wildly. When we managed to calm down, our mood had changed. Elsa stubbornly went back to checking the walls, but the tension had dropped. I was suddenly sure that we weren't going see anything, or find anything at all. It was nothing but an empty house – and Dita had indigestion.

Dita walked around the floor with her arms spread wide. 'What a lot of space. Why do rooms look so much better when they're empty?' She stood by the windows with her arms folded. 'You know, this could be quite a nice house. I'll have it exorcised, and then I think I'll buy it.'

'Too much traffic noise.'

'Double glazing.'

'What about the sunken room?'

She pulled a face. 'Um . . . I'll convert it into a mushroom farm. It's damp enough.'

'I wonder what's causing this,' said Elsa suddenly. She was on her hands and knees on the floor, about a metre from the wall on the street-corner side of the house.

We went to look. 'What is it?' I could see nothing.

'Look at the dust.'

The floor was coated in dust, of course. But the place Elsa was peering at had none. No, it was stranger than that. The dust was there, but it was hanging in the air. A thick horde of dust motes, fizzing like a swarm of tiny silent bees, hovered a few centimetres above the bare boards in a neat clump about the size and shape of a litre juice carton.

'Static electricity,' suggested Dita. 'Static can make your hair stand on end.'

'But why just there?'

We examined the boards carefully, and discovered that the one under the hovering dust had been sawn through. The cut was not fresh, but it didn't look old. The sawn-off part was not nailed down. We used the chisel and screwdriver from my burglarising kit to prise it up.

Underneath the floorboards there was the usual narrow cavity, full of fluff and pipes. At the spot that had been directly under the clean patch there was a box, about the same size as the dust swarm. It was made of some pale wood that had been polished to a fine creamy sheen. I thought I could hear a very faint humming coming from it.

I reached to take it out.

'Are you sure you should do that?'

'Why not?'

Dita had grabbed my arm. Her hand fell. 'I don't know,' she said uncertainly. 'It seems dangerous. As if you might set off an alarm.'

'I'll put it back,' I promised. 'I won't disturb anything.'

My fingers tingled slightly as I touched it. Static electricity, I thought. I wasn't sure what Dita meant by that, but it was a comforting expression. It might explain anything. That or magnetism . . . or possibly both. There was no lock or catch. The lid was a perfect fit, with concealed hinges on one side. It opened easily. Inside there was a metal saucer, which held a pool of yellow liquid. Something like a wax night-light was floating on the surface. Instead of a wick it had a needle like a compass needle, lying across the wax – if it *was* wax. The needle seemed to be made of the same dark metal as the saucer, and it was shifting around quite fast.

I put the box on the floor. We all bent over it.

'Anybody know which way's north?' I asked. (I never know the points of the compass. We've travelled around too much.)

Dita pointed. 'That way. But – what d'you think it is?'

We both looked at Elsa. Don't ask me why.

'It's a control device,' she decided. 'It's for controlling something.'

'Like what?'

'I don't know.'

We crouched there, staring, for a long time. The yellow

liquid gleamed. It looked thick and oily. It was a strange colour, neither acid yellow nor gold, but a mixture of both. The more I looked into it, the more texture and variation I could see. I was tempted to dip my finger in and taste it. The needle went on rocking around, a little less wildly. I tried to remember why I'd insisted on coming to the haunted house. I wanted some evidence, something definite. Instead we'd found only more mystery. But magic is like that, I told myself. It won't behave. I thought of Elsa and her spells. She had it wrong; she'd missed the point, even if the spells seemed to work. Magic is not a set of rules, I decided. It's an entire other world, where unreal things are real.

'Andrei? *Andrei?* Shall we put it back?'

'What?'

I sat back on my heels, shaking my head to clear it. I took Dita's wrist to look at her watch. (I don't wear one. Watches are allergic to me; they won't keep time.) The numbers didn't make sense.

'How long have we been in here?'

'We've been in the house over an hour,' said Dita. 'But we've been staring at that needle for twenty minutes. It seemed to affect you the most. I've been shouting at you.'

Of course when she told me that, I had to look into the box again. The needle had settled; it lay still. I was beginning to study the yellow pool, seeing glints and tiny whorls that I hadn't noticed before . . . when Dita reached out and shut the lid.

'Stop that, Andrei. I think we should put the meditation aid back where we found it before we're stuck here for a week.'

We put the box back, replaced the sawn plank and knelt there blinking at each other. 'How *mysterious!*' exclaimed Dita. None of us could think of anything sensible to add.

'It could be some kind of new drug,' I suggested, not very seriously.

'Or an ouija-compass, that directs you to another world . . .' Dita's eyes were bright. She sounded much happier than she'd been a few minutes before. I could see she was very relieved to have found *something* to justify the way she felt, even if it explained nothing. 'I bet that thing is the cause of the weird atmosphere. We should check the other floors for hidey-holes, now we know what to look for. Do we have time, Elsa?'

Elsa thought about it. 'Not long,' she declared. 'We ought to leave soon.'

I noticed that somewhere along the line Dita had started taking my sister's 'magic' seriously.

'We'll do downstairs,' she said. 'You check the other bedrooms.'

I was glad to be on my own.

I was not surprised that we had not caught any ghosts. According to Mum, my father was alive; and she would know. Though I didn't know how he did his tricks, I was convinced that he was behind everything that had happened. And though we hadn't found a sign of human occupation, I was sure he was using this place. I did not want to find my father here, squatting in a mangy old empty house, plotting misery. I wanted him back in Walsall (or wherever he liked) with his wife and two kids and the fat dog. But if this was how it had to be, then I wanted to get in touch with him. In the end the weird stuff – the chicken-heart eggs, the litter ghosts, that strange compass – did not impress me, somehow. I didn't care if I never found out what it all meant or how the tricks were done. What I wanted was an explanation for the way he'd behaved for so many years, this father I had never met. I wanted to know why he'd been following us around and spying on us, and persecuting my mother.

I wanted to hear his side of the story.

Lots of families break up. Most of them come out the other side of it more or less okay. The parents become friends again after a while. They exchange Christmas cards, invite each other to their parties, share their children without too much heartbreak. Or else one parent, the one who leaves, simply fades, never to be heard of again – which is sad, but it makes life simpler. Why couldn't I be one of the lucky ones?

I went back to the middle bedroom. We'd glanced into it and found nothing, when we first came upstairs. I did not intend to check the floor for hidey-holes. I wasn't interested. It was all right for Dita. Since she'd found a reason for her fright, she could relax and enjoy the haunted-house fun. I had serious business. This was the room that had a lace curtain hanging in the window above the street. I remembered how once I'd seen that curtain shift, as if someone was peering out. There was no sign, but he might use this room.

I took out the photographs I'd brought. One was a recent picture of me. The other was of Mum holding me when I was a baby. There weren't many of those in existence, and I was sorry to part with it. But it was a good cause. I looked for somewhere to put them, and settled on the mantelpiece above the fireplace. I felt as if I was offering a present to an alien chief . . . something of value. I'd decided not to write a note. If he was here, if he was the stalker, then he knew where I lived. The photos were message enough. He could make up his own mind what to do next.

I was staring at my photographs, thinking I'd better go: and make sure the girls didn't come in here again. I didn't want either of them to know what I'd done. The wide sill of the window with the lace curtain caught my eye from across the room. I realised that it could be the lid of a chest. I went over and tried to lift it. It didn't shift. I noticed that below the sill a panel of wood went down to the floor. It was painted the same colour as the rest of the wall, a faded blue, but it looked as if it should be the front of a cupboard. There was no visible catch or keyhole. As I groped about, something shifted. I found I had my fingers in a crack. I got down on my knees and pulled.

The panel slid aside smoothly, though it felt heavy. The cupboard was dark inside. It was dark as a starless night. But I could faintly see, because this darkness had its own kind of light, how the deeps in there stretched away . . . away, into unimaginable space.

I jumped back, like a cat, too startled to make a sound. I couldn't believe it. I peered in again. *It was so dark in there! And it went on forever!* I was kneeling on hard dusty boards, inside the empty house in Roman Road. I had opened a cupboard that couldn't be more than half a metre deep, because further than that would be out through the front wall of the building. Yet I was looking into a vast abyss. It seemed deeper than the deepest ocean, huge as a galaxy. It glowed with brilliant darkness. It was the most beautiful, most terrifying thing I'd ever seen. I wanted to be part of it. The urge to squeeze myself through that narrow door, to fall and fall forever, was so strong I could barely resist it. I remember thinking: *Now I know why this place is called the house of night.*

I didn't dare to put my hand inside. How could I find out if what I saw was real? How could I test it? There was nothing in the room. In desperation I reached up and yanked down the lace curtain. The curtain rod came with it; couldn't have been better. I poked it into the cupboard. How far would it go? Far . . . I hadn't meant to put my hand inside, but finally I had my arm in the dark, almost up to the shoulder, and the end of the curtain rod still hadn't hit anything. My arm felt strange: not exactly cold, not exactly anything. Suddenly the curtain rod . . . well, it *went*. Curtain and hooks and all. I felt it go. I jerked my arm back, afraid I was going to fall into the abyss. My hand was empty.

Footsteps echoed. Someone came running up the uncarpeted stairs. 'Andrei!' called Dita. 'We've found something!' She stood in the doorway, looking straight across the room, into that space of vast dark. 'Oh, another cupboard. Was there anything in it?'

'No,' I said. 'Nothing.' I shut the panel.

'Come and see.'

They'd found a door to the front half of the basement. It was in that dark little lobby by the kitchen. It was locked. Dita shone her torch on the new, shiny fitting.

'So there *is* someone living here.' She frowned. 'I don't know where my psychic feelings fit in, or those weird eggs, but I'm sure ghosts don't put Yale locks on their hideouts.'

'The lock doesn't mean there are no ghosts,' said Elsa obstinately. 'People who can do magic don't use it for ordinary life. Only when they need it.'

We stood looking at the door. I thought of the tools in my daypack, but I didn't want to break in. I was completely bewildered again, because of what I had found in the window chest. I wanted to get away from here; I needed to think.

'What do we do now?' wondered Dita. 'It's your show, Andrei. You say.'

Elsa solved my problem. 'We ought to go,' she announced. 'We've run out of time.'

We left the way we'd got in. I didn't look at the front of the house as we passed it. Elsa did. 'Andrei, what happened to the lace curtain? Did you move it?'

'No. I mean, yes. I don't know what happened to it. Does it matter?'

Dita and my sister had formed an alliance. They looked at each other, raising their eyebrows, silently asking: *Why is he suddenly so grumpy?* I didn't care. I had too much on my mind. I knew that when Dita had walked into the bedroom and looked at that open cupboard, she had not seen what I saw. That black, glittering abyss didn't exist for her. It was only there for me – and I loved it. What on earth did that mean?

Four

*T*HE WEEK AFTER THAT, IT WAS THE EASTER HOLIDAYS. Usually, I didn't like school holidays. We were never going anywhere. I had nothing to do, no money, and I ended up spending too much of my time minding Max and Elsa. This time I was glad of the break. I was even glad to get away from Dita, whose family went off somewhere for a fortnight, taking her with them. It wasn't that she pestered me, but I knew she was wondering about the unsolved mysteries, and expecting to be in on whatever happened next. And I couldn't explain why I had no further plans.

I told myself I was waiting for a message from my father. But that wasn't the whole story. I'd gone to the empty house looking for him; hoping and praying that somehow everything would be explained – that the litter ghosts were some kind of illusion and my father was an ordinary absent-dad with a sad obsession. Now I didn't know what to think. Finding the cupboard full of dark had made things so different. I couldn't convince myself that it had been 'just my imagination', however hard I tried, and it brought the weirdness home to *me*. Anyone can see a ghost, if you believe in such things. But the fact that I could see that shining darkness – and the way I felt about it – seemed to mean there was something strange about me, Andrei. Not my father, not my mother, not my kooky little sister, but me. And I didn't like that. I didn't like it at all.

Family secrets are strange things. I'd never talked to Elsa about the fear man, not directly, before the day Mum had walked us by the empty house on Roman Road. We used to warn each other about Mum's 'bad nerves', and tell each other about signs that 'it was beginning again'. We never discussed *why* Mum was afraid, or why we had to live like this – always on the run, always scared. I suppose I'd thought Elsa was too young to understand. I realised now, from the way she'd behaved since the 'litter ghost' business began, that Elsa understood plenty, in her own way. I wanted to talk to her. I wanted to ask her exactly what she knew, or thought she knew. I wanted to tell her about my discovery in the window chest. But I couldn't. It was like asking Mum about my father: I just couldn't bring myself to begin.

I didn't think too hard about why I felt like this. It seemed obvious. I felt like Dita in the empty house: *this is dangerous, keep away!* The whole topic was like that darkness itself. If I talked about it, or even thought about it too much, I knew I'd have to leap into the beckoning abyss. And I'd be falling, falling forever. Once, in the first week of the holiday, when I was putting them to bed, I tried to sneak up on the subject by questioning Max.

'Remember the grey man, Maxie, who tried to climb our wall? Did you ever see him again?'

Max filled an old baby-wipes container with water and poured it over his ducks. 'No. Poor man, you scared him away, Andry. And he could have been a nice pet.' He looked sad. (Max adores all kinds of animals. He thinks about nothing else but the chance that Mum will one day let us have a pet.) Then he brightened up. 'But there's the big bat.' He flapped his arms. '*Whooo* . . . I like our big bat. You mustn't scare the bat away, will you?'

'*What bat?*'

I didn't know what he was talking about, but a shiver went down my spine. Unfortunately, Max didn't like my tone. He scowled, scooted to the other end of the bath and turned his back on me.

Elsa was at the basin, cleaning her teeth. She'd taken to

going to bed at the same time as Max. It was her own idea, but Mum and I naturally did not object. 'Max?' I said. 'Do you know anything more? Is there something you haven't told me?' But I was looking at Elsa.

She didn't turn around. She kept on brushing her teeth, pretending I didn't exist. I knew she was holding out for a complete surrender. If I wanted her to tell me any more about ghosts and magic. I'd have to ask her directly. But I could not bear to do that.

Something very scary happened a couple of nights later. We had another spook visitor; not the litter ghost – a different one. I hadn't been able to sleep. I hadn't been able to eat my tea either, so I got up, went down and made myself some jam sandwiches. I still didn't feel like eating, but I took them into the living room with a glass of milk, and finally dozed off in front of a late-night film. I woke with a start from a bad dream that I couldn't remember, feeling sure that something was wrong. I crept halfway upstairs, and saw something like a tall, black-winged shadow coming out of the children's room. I don't think I made a sound, but it turned and looked at me. Then it was gone. It had vanished. I rushed up the rest of the stairs and into the room. Max and Elsa were safe. They were peacefully asleep.

I went into my own room and sat on the bed with my head in my hands. I knew I'd glimpsed that eerie shadow before, the night the ghost tried to climb in at the kids' bedroom window. This time I had seen it clearly against the pale outline of the children's bedrom door. I'd seen its eyes, like burning coals. I'd seen the gleam of its teeth, the clawed wings . . . I tried to tell myself I was imagining things, but I knew I wasn't. And then I remembered, with a cold shock, what Max had said about *the big bat*. That was what I'd seen! So we had *another* spooky intruder . . . But this one was worse, because it seemed to have no trouble getting inside the house.

You can bet I didn't sleep at all for the rest of the night.

I tried to keep guard. I stayed awake in my room each night, as long as I could. Every few minutes I'd sneak to the kids' door and check that all was well. I'd go on like that until the dawn. I'd finally fall asleep as it was getting light. Even then I couldn't rest; I dozed, in confused bad dreams. One night I fell asleep downstairs and woke feeling certain something had been in the room. I rushed up the stairs, my heart pounding, and again the shadow was on our landing, black clawed wings towering over its head. I nearly screamed.

'Andrei?'

'It' was gone. My mother stood there, in her old quilted dressing gown.

'Did you see anything?' I gasped. 'I thought there was a burglar.'

She pushed open the children's door. We saw them both, quietly sleeping in the gloom. Mum tucked Elsa's Big Mouse, her favourite soft toy, back under the covers.

'I thought I heard Max. But he's quiet.' She looked into the baby's cot and stroked his hair. 'He's too big for this. We'll have to get him a proper bed. You shouldn't watch tv all night, you know. It's such rubbish. You could read, or do some schoolwork, if you can't sleep. Goodnight.'

I didn't tell her what I thought I'd seen. How could I? It was too crazy.

Easter had been lateish. By the time the holidays ended it was May. I went back to school and tried to behave normally. I usually managed to snatch a nap at lunchtime, on a bench in a discreet corner of the cloakrooms; and if I wasn't very wide awake in class, no one noticed. Fun Day preparations were in full swing. There was generally something going on at the Community Centre. I spent hours there after school, rolling streamers, mending flags, sticking scales on mermaids' tails. It was a wet month. My memory of that time is of us all – Mum and Elsa and Max and me – working away with the Fun Day Committee, while the tea urn hissed and the rain thundered on the flat roof of the hall. The cold, draughty Community Centre was my refuge, it was a place to hide. I thought that was why Mum was there too.

Mum didn't say anything more to me about my sleepless nights, but Mrs Mukarjee noticed that something was wrong. One evening, when I was doing a stack of photocopying in the Community Centre office, she cornered me there with a plate of sandwiches. She wouldn't leave, she said, until I ate. I turned them down. She sucked through her teeth and frowned at me over her glasses as if I was a column of figures that didn't add up. Then she led me to the mirror on the wall.

'Look at that! What is the matter? Anyone would think a vampire had been at you.'

I thought I didn't look bad, considering. But it was true that my face had some interesting purple hollows under the eyes, and my shoulderblades were sticking out as if I was trying to grow wings.

'Nothing's wrong,' I protested. 'I'm sleeping badly, that's all.'

'Very well, very well. Don't explain. But eat!' She shook her head and went away, muttering something about co-education being a silly, overrated western idea. I felt like bursting into tears. She was so kind and concerned. She had no idea.

It's okay, Mrs Mukarjee. I'm not catching anorexia, and I haven't fallen out with your daughter. But you see, my dad has turned out to be the bogey man, and there's this bat-winged ghost that's trying to do something dreadful to my little brother and sister . . .

There was something else: I kept wanting to go back to the house on Roman Road. It grew on me gradually, this

— 71 —

feeling. It got stronger as the days and nights went by. After Mum had gone to her room I'd sneak downstairs again, to keep myself awake by watching tv – and I'd sit there thinking about the house of night. Not about my cupboard full of darkness; just the house itself. *Got to go back there. Everything'll work out if I go back there.* My thoughts went on like that. Of course I wasn't going to go. I knew it was a trap. But I couldn't stop thinking about it . . .

The tv ploy didn't work very well. (In fact, I would recommend any one of the old films they put on at 2am as a sure-fire cure for insomnia.) One night I fell asleep and dreamed that a litter ghost had come to fetch me. In my dream, I was lying on our dark green couch, my head squished against the worn patch on the left-hand arm. The tv had gone blank in front of me and was humming its dead, middle-of-the-night tune. I turned my head and I saw the grey ghost forming out of nothing. The mouth in its blank clown face moved, though no sound came out. It stretched its skinny arms and beckoned . . . I started awake, sitting bolt upright with my heart thumping. I sat there until I was breathing normally again. Then I went very quietly up the stairs to check on Max and Elsa. The door to their room was open. That was funny – I was sure it had been shut. I looked in.

It was bending over Elsa's bed.

The bat-thing was leaning down over my little sister, in a horrible parody of the way I'd seen Mum lean down to kiss the kids when they were asleep. I saw its fangs. I saw its blood-red eyes and the black cloak of folded wings. Mrs Mukarjee had said the word that leapt into my head: *vampire.* I must have made some kind of noise, some wail of horrified helplessness. Next instant, it leapt into the air. The shroud of darkness that hung around it opened . . . and I ran across the room. Too late. The thing had jumped *through* a closed window.

I couldn't see anything outside. I checked the kids. They

were alive and breathing normally; they didn't seem harmed. I ran downstairs and out into the back garden. It was raining. There was no sign of the intruder. I ran back through the house. I wasn't thinking very clearly. I wasn't thinking at all, in fact. I saw a shadow blacker than the darkness flying away from me down the street, and I raced after it. It turned a corner, and another. I followed, pounding along with the rain driving in my face. I was not going to lose it. I was going to catch the shadow, the way I'd caught the grey man, the fear man's servant. I was going to tear it to pieces. I kept running . . . until a body loomed ahead of me. I tried to dodge, too late. I skidded, lost my footing on the slippery pavement, and crashed to the ground.

'Andrei! Andrei, what on earth were you doing?'

My mother helped me up. I'd winded myself. I could only gasp. 'I was— I was—'

'What's going on? I heard you yell. I came out of my room and found the front door wide open. You left the back door open too. What happened? What's got into you?'

I stood there gulping like a fish, the rain pelting me, struggling to make sense of her arrival. How had I run into her if she was chasing *after* me?

'I was chasing an intruder,' I gasped. 'At least, I thought there was . . . someone . . . something. I'm sorry I left the doors open.'

I looked around me. I was surprised to find that I wasn't even near our house. We were halfway to the High Street, on one of the street corners at the edge of Elsa's old circle of protection. 'I didn't realise I'd come this far,' I mumbled.

'You must have been running with your eyes shut,' said Mum. 'I had to get in front of you to stop you. You didn't see me pass you. Didn't you hear me calling?'

That was strange. I was sure no one had run past me. I

was sure no one had been calling. Even her voice sounded strange. But I couldn't argue with her, I was too bewildered. I looked away, into the dark wet streets, towards the house on Roman Road. I could feel it pulling me. I'd have to go . . .

'Andrei? *Andrei!*'

She was shaking my arm. 'Wake up. Let's go home. We're getting soaked.'

We headed back. My heart was still pounding and my throat hurt. I was very confused. I'd lost the thread of what was happening completely. I'd thought that the bat-thing must have been sent by the same enemy that sent the litter ghosts. But I didn't know any more where my father fitted in. Or a cupboard full of dark . . . Mum said nothing. Now that I'd calmed down enough to notice it, I was cold and wet and uncomfortable. My tracksuit was sticking to my shoulders. But walking in the dark soothed me. It felt strangely like one of our old night walks. I took courage from that.

'Mum,' I began, 'there *was* an intruder. Didn't you see anything? You must have done. I've s-seen it before. It's not . . . it's not an ordinary burglar.' That sounded so lame. I'd have to tell her what I'd seen. But she'd think I was crazy. Bat wings, red eyes, fangs . . .

She stopped, and I did too. 'Where were you going, Andrei?'

I noticed – I hadn't thought of it before – that she was fully dressed. Of course, Mum was often up in the middle of the night, prowling around. She was a nocturnal animal. I didn't understand her question. It didn't seem to make sense.

'I wasn't going anywhere. I told you. I was chasing the . . . thing.' I didn't want to describe it. 'The thing I thought I saw. I don't know, maybe I was dreaming. I've been having bad dreams. But Mum, there *is* someone spying on us. You know that. Always has been, for years and years.

It's my father, isn't it. You don't have to tell me; I've found out for myself. What does he want, Mum? What's going on? I can't sleep, I have horrible dreams – visions, almost, about imaginary monsters . . . Do I sound crazy? I feel as if I'm going crazy.'

She stopped walking and sat down on the low wall of someone's front garden.

'Andrei, have you been back to the haunted house? Elsa's haunted house?'

I couldn't understand these questions. *Where were you going? Have you been back to the house?* Why was she going on about that house? I'd been chasing a monster.

'No. Of course not.'

I lied by instinct, without thinking. I could tell she didn't believe me.

'*Did you leave anything there?*' she demanded, urgently.

'No! I told you, I haven't been near the place. Why should I?'

I was blushing in the dark, thinking of those photographs. Luckily she didn't see. After a moment she stood up, without speaking, and we went on. But I'd steeled myself somehow to talk about our problem, and I wasn't going to give up this time.

'Mum,' I began, 'we have to face him some time. We have to stop running.'

'I did stop running,' she said then, bleakly. I couldn't tell if it was rain on her cheeks, or tears. 'There's not much time left; we have to sort things out at last. That's why we're here. But I was wrong; it's too dangerous. We have to get away. Andrei, I'll explain everything soon, when we're safely away. I swear I will. Meanwhile, do not go back there. Do you hear me? *Don't go near that house again.*'

I knew from her tone that I wasn't going to get any more answers. We reached home in silence. Mum went straight to her room and shut the door. I stripped off my wet clothes, crawled into bed and fell at once into a dreamless sleep.

I woke up in the morning feeling better, physically. But I knew something drastic had happened. When I came home from school, there were national papers on the table in our dining-nook. Mum was sitting with the telephone, listening to someone on the other end, nodding and saying *Yes, yes*, occasionally. I saw the dreaded circles drawn in red ink under Situations Vacant. She put down the phone and gathered her newspapers together. She didn't speak and neither did I. We were back where we'd been before. I'd told her too much, last night out in the rain. She'd had enough of our enemy: of bad dreams and monsters. We were off again – another job, another town, another miserable uprooting. And she wasn't going to talk about it.

She started waiting for me at the school gates, as if I was five years old. I'd come out with the crowd and find her there, looking defiant, with Elsa in tow and Max in his buggy. I didn't complain, though it was embarrassing. Then she told me she didn't want me to go to Agnelli's any more. In fact, I wasn't to go anywhere on my own. We were to stick together until she could organise the move. We stopped going to the Community Centre. We stayed at home, Mum in her CIA fugitive mode, setting up a new life over the phone.

For days I accepted everything. I didn't argue, I didn't protest, I didn't even ask where we were going. She probably wouldn't have told me. She'd always been very secretive when she was planning a flight. Then one evening, I came down from my room about seven, and casually slung my jacket over my shoulders.

'I'm going round to Dita's, Mum. I need some Maths notes.' I walked out, quickly, before she could react.

I actually did go round to Dita's. I'd been avoiding her at school and I felt bad about it. I owed her an explanation; and there might not be many more chances for us to meet alone. The way my mother worked, I wouldn't have much notice when moving day came. Mr Mukarjee let me in with a big smile. He fetched Dita down from her bedroom (he called it her 'study'), and left us to talk in the dining room with the big polished table, where I used to share their Sunday lunch. I thought *used to*, because I knew it wouldn't happen again. The table was covered in seashell hats, and strips of blue and green crêpe paper.

'I'm sorry your mother's not going to do her show after all,' began Dita, in a stilted, polite way. 'It's a shame she's too busy.'

My Mum must have told the Fun Day people something, I didn't know what. 'She's too busy getting a new job,' I said. 'We're leaving. I'm probably not supposed to tell you; she likes to keep things secret. But you'll find out soon, anyway. We're off again, me and Mum and the kids.'

'Oh!' Her stiff, polite expression melted. 'Is *that* what's been wrong? Thank goodness. I thought you suddenly hated me . . .' Then she looked bewildered. 'But Andrei, what about your father? And the haunted house, and all that business?'

I shrugged. 'Yeah, well. Mum says she's going to explain everything. After we've moved.' I wanted to say something that began: *If this is goodbye . . .* or *Don't forget me.* But I knew it was no good, and I couldn't get the words out anyway.

'Maybe she wants you to hear her side of the story first.'

But Mum had had plenty of time for that, and she'd told me nothing.

'I'm going back to the house,' I announced, abruptly. 'She's made me swear not to go near it, but I'm going there tonight, to knock on the basement door. I'm going to have it out with him, I hope. I wanted you to know, I'm taking your advice at last. I thought you'd be proud of me.'

We didn't talk much more. I picked up the Maths notes

(which, supposing my school career meant anything at all, I genuinely did need) and left.

Five

I WENT IN OVER THE GATE IN THE ALLEY, AS BEFORE. Nothing had changed, except that the garden was a riot of flowering weeds, and the briars that blocked the path were covered in small, mildewed, crimson rosebuds. I walked round them. It was about nine o'clock on a cool May evening, and still more or less daylight. Inside, the house seemed gloomy by contrast, but I had no trouble picking my way through the kitchen rubble.

The new lock gleamed on the basement door. I stood looking at it for a minute, making up my mind. Then I crept away as quietly as I could. A strange feeling of longing had come over me. I wanted to know if the panel under the window would open again. I remembered that glittering darkness, like deep water. I wanted to stare into it again, to let my mind fall away into that secret night – just for a moment, and then I would go to meet my father.

The middle bedroom was silent and empty. I could see the holes in the window frame, where I had torn down the curtain rod. I could remember the way it felt when I put my hand and arm into the blackness. So strange! When we came ghost hunting, Dita had said the house made her feel sick. I didn't feel sick, far from it, but this time I felt something. I was tingling all over. But not with fear! It felt more like pure excitement.

Hold on, I thought, suddenly. *This is not good.*

I was supposed to be here to confront my father, and all I could think about was that cupboard. I stood in the middle of the bare room, debating. Why had I come back? Was it really to see my father, or was it the house itself that had drawn me? I didn't trust this thing, that could make me feel like a drug addict hungry for a fix. But how could I be sure that what I remembered was real unless I had another look? I told myself that it would do no harm if I tried to open the panel, to see if there was anything there . . .

'Hi, Andrei, ' said a voice behind me.

I spun around. There was a man standing in the doorway. He was average height, not much taller than me. He was bone–thin and dressed in casual, shabby clothes. He had a little beard. Under it, in the open collar of his shirt, I could see a puckered, purplish scar, or maybe it was a birthmark. But for someone whose lifestyle involved squatting in an empty house and stalking his ex–wife and her kids, he didn't look bad. You'd have passed him on the street without noticing him.

'I see you know about the night–window.' He had a soft, pleasant, Caribbean accent. I was surprised at that. I'd sort of assumed he would be English–born, but of course there was no reason why he should be.

I'd been kneeling in front of the panel. I was on my feet again now.

He walked into the room and sat down cross-legged on the boards in front of the fireplace. He took a packet of tobacco, papers and matches from his pocket and began to make himself a cigarette. I noticed that he had the same kind of scars on his wrists as he had on his throat, as if he'd once been badly burned.

'You want a roll–up?'

'I don't smoke.'

'Good.' He nodded, lighting up and puffing. 'I'm glad you don't smoke.'

I glanced, without meaning to, at the mantelpiece where I'd left the photographs. They were gone. He caught my eye and smiled, a secretive smile.

'You're a nice–looking boy.' He jerked his head at the window–panel. 'You're interested in that. Of course you are. Strange things happen in this house, Andrei. They always have, in this house and in this place before the house was here.'

'What is it?' I asked. 'The thing you call the night-window, what is it?'

He pondered. 'Mmm. Maybe you could call it a matter–transmitter. Things that you drop in there vanish, and they appear somewhere else. You can climb into it, or through it, and step out on the other side of the world or in the middle of next week.'

The idea of *climbing into* that darkness stirred my longing again. But it sounded funny. I thought of falling into utter night. I saw myself looking stupid, kicking on the floor with my head in a cupboard. My resistance to weirdness woke up. This man was real, solid and ordinary. I wasn't going to be taken in by any wild stories.

'I don't believe it.'

'Not everybody can do the trick.' He stared at me, shook his head and gave a dry little laugh. 'I've been wasting my time, Andrei. All these years. I didn't need to trail around, keeping an eye on her. I might have known. She had to come back. All I had to do was stay here and wait until the time came. But I didn't want to lose touch, you know?'

He grimaced, pointing his roll–up round at the bare walls. 'What a dump! You must think I'm crazy, camping out in this place. But it wasn't like this in the old days. It was cosy; it was the clubhouse. It was hopping with fun, all kinds of people, parties . . . We used to have good times in this house, me and Mili. This is where we met. Did she ever tell you that?'

'No.'

He was watching my face carefully. 'She hasn't told you anything,' he decided. He sounded pleased, like a theory of his had been proved, and relieved.

I didn't answer. I didn't know what to say. He stood up,

in one easy movement. I saw that he was wiry and trim, I suddenly thought he might be very strong.

'Let's go downstairs. I'll make you a cup of tea. We've a lot to talk about.'

I won't pretend I felt malevolent vibes. Definitely, I am not psychic. But I knew I didn't want to go with him.

'*Are* you my father?'

I thought we were taking far too much for granted.

He gave an impatient frown, as if I'd mentioned something completely irrelevant. Which was strange, because that was the reason we were here, surely. Because he was my father, because he wanted to tell me his side of the story.

'You could say that,' he admitted. 'Come on, Andrei. Downstairs.'

I didn't want to go downstairs. It struck me that he was talking to me as if I was a dog or something. As if he expected to be obeyed. I didn't feel like obeying him. Yet he was certain that I would, so certain he wasn't even bothering to coax me or put on much of a long-lost Daddy act. I suppose he guessed I wouldn't be impressed by sentiment, after all that had happened. Suddenly a wash of pure fear went through me, the kind of fear that jumps out and grabs you before your conscious mind knows why. But though the thin man was so sure I would do what I was told, I didn't feel compelled. I wasn't going to go down to his lair.

As I decided this, I realised exactly what I had done in coming here. *I had answered his summons.* Suddenly I understood that this was what had frightened Mum when she found me out in the dark, running *towards Roman Road.* She'd known that I was being pulled here, that I couldn't resist. That's why she'd decided we had to run away again. And now he'd got me, after all. He had me here alone, which was what he'd always wanted . . .

But I could escape if I could reach the window into

night. I stood there, between two forces, understanding for the first time that there *were* two forces, both tugging at me. I didn't know why, but I felt that the night-window was not to be feared. It was my longing for the night that was pulling against this smiling, dangerous stranger, and keeping me from being forced to obey him. Something in my eyes must have given me away. I saw *his* eyes sharpen. He threw down the end of his roll–up and put his hand to his stubbly hollow cheek. He brought it away, like a conjuror who reaches behind your ear and brings out a coin. He was holding something. He kneaded it for a moment with his fingers against his palm, and then tossed it to the floor. It was a chicken–heart egg. In that cold room I could feel a faint, animal-innards warmth rising from it. Newborn, it was covered in a film of slime, like spit.

It didn't lie still for more than a second. It opened and a ghost burst silently out – another creature like the one I'd chased in the High Street, the one I'd fought, the figure that had plagued me in dreams. It was a limp, sketchy thing made of grey rot, rubbish, and dirt; of unwanted, discarded things. It was born crouched, its face and arms splayed flat on the boards. It clambered to its knees, the head still hanging loosely. Grey fingers quivered towards me.

'You don't know what's going on, Andrei. I can see that. Come with me and I'll explain.'

'No,' I cleared my throat, and tried again, 'No!' I managed to say it louder this time. 'It can't hurt me. I don't know how you make them seem alive, but it's a trick to frighten children. I'm not afraid.'

The grey thing swayed on the floor between us, its papery limbs thickening.

'Not afraid? Well, you ought to be. You're right, my puppets can't do much, not the standard model. But it's different if I've had personal material to work into the spell. They're like bloodhounds. They need a hook, a handle, something to give them the scent. If I can feed 'em something like that, then they have plenty of bite.'

'You haven't got anything of mine!'

Then I remembered the photographs I'd left here; and how my mother had asked me so urgently that night in the rain, *did you leave anything?* I knew I'd been very stupid.

He grinned and shrugged, shamefacedly. 'Yeah. I see you understand. I'm sorry about your souvenirs, but I didn't have any choice. I need your help, Andrei. I need it *badly*. I don't want to hurt you, but I can't take any chances. I've been waiting too long. So come on. No more messing about. Be sensible'.

The ghost raised its head. It did not have the same blank clown–face as the others. It had teeth, and there was a dull, horrible gleam in its eyes.

I can't tell you very clearly what happened next. I know I yelled, 'No!' and made a dive for the window. Something lashed out, and I fell over. The ghost had decked me. I managed to fight free . . . but not quite. There was a moment when I was sprawled half on my knees. It had hold of me by one ankle, and I was trying to crawl to the window, which was suddenly miles away. It was gripping so hard I thought it would pull my foot off.

There was another moment when *something else* came into the room in a rush. I thought it was another ghost, that the stranger (I couldn't believe he was really my father) had called up to finish me off. I screamed, because it was the bat–winged creature with the red eyes: the monster I'd seen bending over Elsa as she slept, its fangs almost at her throat. I cowered away from the swirl of dark wings. But it didn't attack me. It turned on the thin man. It was grappling with him, shaking him, the way the dark night wind takes and shakes a rag of litter. *Oh no, I thought. He's lost control of his own tricks, it'll kill him and then turn on me, I haven't a chance* . . . I saw him fall, and the thing leapt

—— 84 ——

towards me. It was just *swoosh!* Darkness everywhere. At that point, I fainted.

'Andrei? *Andrei?*'

I was waking up from a nightmare. I lay without opening my eyes, feeling the normal world come back and thinking gratefully, *Thank God that wasn't true* . . . Gradually it dawned on me that my head wasn't on a pillow. It was on hard boards. I was lying on the dusty floor in the bedroom in the empty house. My head was aching like mad and my right ankle seemed to be on fire. I opened my eyes and saw Dita looking down at me.

'Are you all right?'

'What happened?' I asked. I was too muzzy to be surprised that she was there.

She held my head still and looked into my eyes: she was checking for concussion, I guessed. 'I told your mother,' she confessed. 'I'm sorry Andrei, but you said you were coming back here, alone, to confront your father. I thought someone ought to know.' She seemed to be in a state of shock herself. Her face looked grey, I could feel her shaking.

'Someone attacked me,' I muttered, half sitting up. I didn't know what she'd seen; I wondered if she'd seen anything at all. There was no sign of the grey ghost, or that other terrible creature. There was only the empty room, grown very shadowy.

'Where is he?' I couldn't say 'my father'. 'That man?'

'He got away,' said my mother's voice.

She was there too, kneeling beside me. She pushed my shoulders gently back down to the floor. 'He got away,' she repeated. 'Lie down. Rest a moment. You've had a bad shock.'

'Mum, is it true? *Was* that my father?'

She stroked my hair. 'Lie still. Don't worry about it now.'

'Was there anyone else here, besides him, when you came?'

'No. There was no one else.'

I wanted to insist on telling my mother the truth before the 'real world' took over again and I lost my certainty. But Dita was examining the place where the ghost had grabbed me. It hurt unbelievably. I couldn't speak, I could only chew down a moan.

'I'm sure this ankle's broken, Mrs Chapman,' Dita announced, sounding faint and strained. 'I'd better go and find a phone. I'll call a taxi – or an ambulance?'

'No,' answered Mum. 'He'll be all right; we can manage. You should go home. And thank you, Dita. Thank you more than I can say.'

That was typical of my mother. I knew she wouldn't take me near a hospital. She was terrified of hospitals, the same way she was terrified of anything remotely 'official'. I could only hope the ankle wasn't as bad as it felt. Dita was staring at Mum with eyes like saucers. From the look on her face I felt sure that *she* had seen the whole show. But then why wasn't she jabbering about ghosts and winged demons?

She didn't say anything like that. She picked up her Maths notes, which were lying on the floor, and shuffled them back into their folder. 'I'll help you to get him home.'

I thought Mum would refuse. It was so hard for my mother to accept any kind of help. But she didn't. 'Thank you,' she smiled. 'That would be good.' I reached up and took hold of her hands. They were warm. She squeezed mine in a comforting grip.

'How do you feel now?' she asked. 'Shall we see if you can stand up?'

They helped me to limp down the stairs. I was dizzy, and maybe that deadened the pain, because it wasn't too bad. The two of them had managed to force the front door, apparently, when they rushed to the rescue. The junk mail was scattered up the passageway, its murky spell broken. The door had swung shut. It was stuck again. As Dita wrestled it open, my mother and I both turned to look up the hall towards the lobby by the kitchen, where the basement door was lurking with its shiny new lock. *He got away,* my mother had said. I knew – though I couldn't imagine the scene – that she had let him go. But he hadn't gone far. He was down there now, in his lair. I could feel it. She didn't say anything, neither did I.

Dita found us a taxi and paid for it. I remember thinking, *that's going to cause trouble.* Mum would insist on paying her her back and Dita would refuse; and Mum would get in a state. I was very worried about that social difficulty. It is amazing how your mind keeps on playing its old worn–down tracks, when everything is falling apart. The taxi driver didn't seem to notice anything strange. We reached our house without saying much.

As soon as we were indoors, Dita said, 'I'll make some coffee. I'm sure I can find things.' She rushed off into the kitchen.

Mum helped me upstairs. She took me into her own room, and sat me down on the stool in front of the old pine chest she used as a dressing table, with my back to the triple mirror that stood on top. She left me. I heard a murmur of voices. I was shocked to realise that the kids had been alone. Elsa had been in charge, obviously. I could hear the pride in her sleepy voice, as she reported her *All's well.* My mother came back. I thought she'd brought me up here to treat my ankle. I was waiting for her to fetch out the medicine box, where she kept plasters and dressings and the few herbal remedies that she would allow us to use. Arnica tablets – I've chewed more arnica tablets in my time than any other living teenager . . .

'What's wrong with Dita?' I asked, kind of testing the water.

'Not a lot. I like your girlfriend, Andrei. She's very sensible and very brave.'

It was the first time I'd heard anybody call Dita Mukarjee 'sensible'. But Mum was changing the subject and I couldn't allow that. 'She saved my life, didn't she? You two saved my life. I was a fool to go there alone. I'm sorry. But Mum, you *have to* explain everything now. About my father, and the ghost–puppets, and the other thing, the bat–winged monster. Don't tell me I didn't see those creatures. Don't say it isn't real. I have to face these things, at last. I've seen that monster in our house. I think you know all about it. If you say I'm imagining things, I'll *really* go crazy.'

I said this all in a rush, before common sense could intervene and keep me quiet. My mother sat on her bed. She had a strange expression, almost laughing; and yet she looked as if she was going to cry.

'You want to know the truth?'

I drew a deep breath. 'Yes.'

'Andrei, ' she sighed. 'My baby.'

The look in her eyes suddenly terrified me. I knew then, at that moment, that I'd been lying. I *didn't* want to know. I hadn't kept silent all these years for nothing – looking the other way, refusing to notice anything strange. *I didn't want to know.* I wanted the world back the way it was before: ghosts and monster shut away where they couldn't reach me. But it was too late. The wall between real and unreal had begun to collapse the first day that I saw that house on Roman Road.

My mother moved, like someone shaking back their hair or shaking off a spray of water. I saw her change. She was still herself, I could still recognize her. She was also – unbelievably and yet it was true – the monster I had seen haunting our house: the bat–winged shadow–creature with fangs and terrible eyes.

'What are you?' I quavered.

'I'm your mother, ' said the shadow in my mother's voice. 'Believe that. It's the truth. But what you're looking at now is also me. This is the way I am. You have heard about creatures like me. You've heard the stories. I'm a monster, a creature of darkness, the undead. That's what I'm called. But try to see beyond. Try—'

So I tried. What did I see? It's hard to put into words. The best way I can explain it is to say that my brain saw something it could not describe to me. So it was frightened, and it borrowed scraps from all its images of *fear*. It patched them together, and told me: *This is what you see.* I knew, because I was staring right at her this time, that there were no leathery clawed bat wings, no fangs. The aura of shining darkness around her wasn't wings at all. It was some other sort of extension: a kind of flickering margin between her and the normal world – this bedroom. The monster impression was still there in my mind, but it was like a thin overlay over something much more strange, something utterly *not* . . . I saw something that wasn't of this world. I couldn't really tell you more than that. And yet I saw a person. My mother. It was still her.

'H – have you always been like this, Mum?'

A fierce tension went out of the shadow creature as soon as I spoke. I felt I'd passed some kind of test, or we had passed it together. I realised, in the middle of my own panic, how terrified she must have been of telling me the truth. She did that shaking thing again, sort of backwards, and looked like my normal mum again.

'Always.' She suddenly laughed, daffy with relief. 'No one bit me, no one cursed me, I didn't take the witch's apple. I was born this way.'

She settled herself and drew a long breath. I knew she must have rehearsed for this moment a hundred million times. 'I was born this way,' she repeated. 'I was born in a little country far away from here, a tiny country buried in the Caucasus mountains, near to the Black Sea. It's very isolated. When my grandmother was a little girl, there were still people in my country who talked a kind of Latin and thought there was an emperor ruling in Rome. That's how far away from the world we were.'

'And everyone was like you?'

'Not at all. Only a few people were born this way, in certain families. It was something we tried to keep secret, because there was prejudice. One of my grandmothers was like me. She taught me a lot before she died. The rest of my family were fairly normal.' She smiled, remembering. 'As normal as families ever are—'

I was struggling to take it in 'So, it's like a hereditary disease?'

'You could say that. But we're not sick. We're *different* at a very basic level, below the molecular. You could say we're infected with the immaterial, with the other side of things, the opposite of the "ordinary reality" of human bodies and rocks and earth and anything you can touch. It means we can do things other people can't do. We can see in the dark, walk through walls, fly – at least it feels like flying, though it's not like a bird. We can be invisible. We call ourselves, as far as we have a name we agree on, the night people. Ordinary life belongs to the day. We belong to night and darkness, if only because we've always had to hide. But you know, Andrei, that most of the universe is made of darkness. I've told you about that. We are not aliens – we belong. On a cosmic scale, maybe *we're* the normal ones, and the rest of planet earth is out of step. It's a comforting thought. We like it.'

'Are you . . . immortal? Have you lived for hundreds of years?'

She laughed. 'No! Nothing so romantic. Though actually, I don't think I'd like that. We live as long as other people, or not much longer. But there is something behind those stories of "the undead" coming back from their graves. Until we're very old, we can recover from terrible injuries or fatal illness. It sometimes doesn't happen until after clinical death. I told you, my grandmother – my father's mother – was like me. When she was sixteen years old, she *died* of TB. It was a common illness in my country then; it still is, I believe. Her family knew what she was and kept her body unburied for days, but in the end they had to give up hope. She woke in her coffin in the churchyard. Luckily for her, it was winter. She wasn't buried. She woke in the charnel–house with the other winter's dead, where they were waiting to be buried in the Spring, and came in her grave clothes, knocking at her parents' door in the middle of the night. You can imagine what kind of a reception she would have had from the rest of the village, if her family hadn't protected her. You've seen the movies.'

Yes, I'd seen the movies. I saw in my mind a white-faced girl, like my mother; with a stake through her heart. My whole body prickled with dread.

'Do you drink human blood?' I blurted.

I know it was awful, but I was not in a state to be polite. She winced.

'I want to be honest with you, Andrei. I don't want to hide anything. You've heard of vampires, werewolves, voodoo-demons. There are legends about "monsters" like that all over the world. I believe that all the different names are really names for people like me. And some of the most frightening stories *are probably true*. Night people can live in bizarre ways, evil ways, and some of them do. Being severely different from everybody around you is not good for the soul. Some of us are very nasty indeed. Which makes us even with the rest of the human race, as far as I can see.'

I nodded. The prickles had turned into a kind of inner shivering. Buried alive! The cold of that winter night in the mountains seemed to have invaded my mother's bed-room.

'Let me tell you the rest of my history. Things were very

bad in my country when I was growing up. We weren't as isolated as we once had been, but we might as well have been the slaves of a wicked Roman Emperor, the kind of life we had to live. My mother and father were in trouble with the police, and they were afraid for me, because I'm different. They managed to send me abroad. I came to this country to study – to this very city. I wanted to study basic science, so I could understand what kind of creature I was. I worked hard, but I also met other people like me. There are a few of us in most cities, it seems. It was wonderful to have friends. I met your father, and we fell in love, and you were born.' She stopped. When she began again her words were like fingertips, painfully touching a sore place. 'Then we fell out. It was a bad break–up. I left him, I ran away . . . '

'Why didn't you *tell* me all this?' I burst out.

She spread her hands, helplessly. 'I wanted you to have a childhood. And to have a choice, the choice I never had. When we found Alan, I thought we were safe. He didn't know. As far as he was concerned, I was a normal person. I was careful and we were happy, weren't we? But Alan died, and I know that since then I haven't been good to you. I was trying to spare you from the hurt and trouble. But I spoiled your life; I know I did.'

'Oh no,' I said, as quickly as I could. 'No – you never did that!'

Imagine me, sitting there with my eyes popping and my mouth open. I couldn't take in her apology. There was plenty she still needed to explain, but everything else seemed trivial beside the main news. My mother is a vampire! My blood had curdled into icy soup. It was managing to crawl around somehow, but not much of it was getting to my brain.

'And my father?' I croaked. '*Was* that my father? In the house?'

'I'm afraid it was.'

'Is he like you?'

She winced again. 'Not exactly. That was the problem . . . I told you, being this way is hereditary. But there are degrees of inheritance. The children of night people and humans are sometimes fully one thing or the other, and sometimes hybrids. Your father's one of those, the inbetweens; like Elsa. He's a kind of magician.'

'Those chicken–heart things', I swallowed a lump of disgust that jumped into my throat at the memory, 'that hatch into the litter ghosts. That's his magic. But are they real, or is it some kind of illusion? How does he do it?'

'It's called ectoplasm. I don't think anybody knows how it works, but magicians can pull that goop out of themselves and use it in their magic; sometimes to animate the puppets they send on their errands. I'm not sure what you mean by "illusion". Those things are as real as ill-will. But they can't do much harm, unless the magician has something belonging to the victim, to intensify the spell.'

'I left him some photographs. He used them, to give the chicken–heart egg ghost some teeth.' I was feeling sorely confused. 'But Mum,' I cried accusingly, 'You told me my father was normal. You said he was "a very normal man"!'

She stared at me in surprise. 'Did I say that? Yes, I remember, I did. I'm sorry, I didn't mean to deceive you. It was a . . . a bitter comment. My problem with your father is not that he's a magician. He's not wicked because he's different – that's no excuse.' Her eyes flashed. 'The way he's behaving is just like any "normal" man, the kind of man who thinks his woman is his property. He can't believe it's over between us. He thinks I have to do what he says and give him what he wants, no matter what.'

'All right, all right. I get it.' But my staggering brain caught up with something else she'd told me. 'Wait a minute . . . *Elsa's* a magician?' I was disgusted, in the midst of this shattering conversation. It was true her 'spells' had sometimes seemed to work, but I'd hoped that would turn out to be a coincidence. She'd be unbearable when she knew.

Mum grinned weakly at my expression. 'I'm afraid so, Andrei. And we're lucky she's on our side. Whereas my dear sweet Max is completely . . . well, what people call normal.' She sat and looked at me. She seemed to have run out of words. My brain was churning and teeming with questions, but I couldn't sort out which I wanted to ask.

'I trusted him,' she said at last. 'I mean Ross, your father. The inbetweens are fascinated by the night people. Some of them envy us and hate us; but they can't leave us alone. When I met Ross I thought he wasn't like the others. I thought he loved me. But it was my power he wanted, or what he sees as "power". He couldn't accept that it wasn't like money. I couldn't write a cheque and hand it over. In the end he stole something from us, from you and me. He found he couldn't use this thing he stole, and then he was angry. He started to treat me badly, so I took you and ran away. We've been running ever since.'

I looked around my mother's sanctum. The curtains were open. The quiet glow of night–time, so much easier on the eye than daylight, gleamed on the midnight blue shawl which was slung over a chair by her bed, and on the black and silver quilt-cover she'd sewn herself from some other old-country material . . .

'I'll see what's happened to Dita,' I said, when the silence had grown too long.

I found her in the kitchen. She'd put three mugs on a tin tray. The kettle had boiled; it was still steaming. That was as far as she'd got. She was standing with her arms wrapped round her as if she was freezing, staring bug–eyed at the cupboards above our kitchen counter. The fridge hummed loudly.

'You've talked to my mother?' I began, not sure how much she knew.

'Yeah,' she said mechanically, without turning round.

'We had a long talk while you were unconscious. You were out for I don't know how long; it seemed like ages. She wasn't worried, not then . . . I had to tell her, Andrei. From the things you'd told me, I thought your father – if it was your father – could be dangerous. I didn't know what to say on the phone. So I rushed over here, and then we rushed over to the empty house. We couldn't find a taxi and the buses are useless; it was frantic. She was terrified, and that scared me even more. We arrived there and she shoved open that front door – *Wham!* No problem! She's *strong.* We heard voices. She flew up the stairs. Flew! It was nearly dark but I could see. I saw her. She was . . . she was . . . ' Dita swallowed hard and tried again. 'Well, you know what she was. I ran after her. She had that man by the throat and you were lying on the floor. I thought you were dead. She shoved him past me, out of the room. I don't know where he went. Then she was your mother, a normal person again—'

'So you know,' I said, when I could get a word in edgeways. 'No wonder you were looking weird when I came round. I don't think it's sunk in with me. I'm waiting to wake up.' I started to laugh, overcome with relief at having someone with me, someone to share this terrifying experience. I was thinking, *There's one good thing about all of this.* Whatever happened, I'd never have to worry again about having a girlfriend who was too whacky to fit in with my sensible life. '*My mother is a vampire!* I can't believe it!'

Then at last she turned that bug-eyed stare on me, full blast.

'Andrei. It's not your mother I'm worried about.'

'Huh?'

'How's your ankle? It was broken an hour ago. *There was a piece of bone sticking out through your skin.*'

Then the truth finally hit me. I rushed out of the kitchen. I took the stairs three at a time. (The broken ankle was fine, since you ask.) She was sitting where I'd left her, waiting.

Waiting, the way she'd been waiting for years, for me to start asking those questions.

So I asked. 'What about me? I look human, I feel human. *What am I?*'

She came over to me and took my hands. 'Andrei,' She said gravely, 'That's exactly what we have to talk about. There's more to the story. It's time for you to hear it all.'

Six

SOMETHING BUMPED AGAINST THE DOOR. IT WAS DITA, with three mugs of coffee. She smiled at us nervously, and set down the tray on the floor. She looked at my mother.

'I brought the sugar. I know about Andrei. Do you take masses too?'

'Yes, thanks.' Mum glanced at me. 'That's one benefit. There are some physical differences in all night-people's children.' She grinned. 'We don't get tooth decay.'

My teeth! Goodness. I reached my tongue around the front of my mouth, wondering if I'd feel my eye-teeth growing into Dracula-fangs. I almost burst into hysterical laughter. It couldn't be true. Not me. I must be normal, like Max, or nearly normal. My mother must have fixed my ankle herself with her super-powered touch.

'I sometimes thought he might be diabetic,' muttered Dita. 'Always hungry, always tired and pale, always rubbing his eyes as if he couldn't see properly.'

'I don't!'

'Yes, you do.'

'It's that strip lighting they use at school and in Agnelli's. It's too strong; it messes up the colours of everything.'

'No it doesn't, Andrei.'

Mum coughed politely. 'Do you two want to hear the rest of the story?'

'I do!' cried Dita instantly. 'Why is Andrei's father after you? And what's the house got to do with it? And how are we going to sort you out, you and Andrei's dad?' She hesitated. 'I'm sorry, that sounds cheeky. But there must be a solution.'

Trust Dita. See bad situation, solve bad situation. She'd been longing to get stuck into my mother's problem life, practically since the day she and I met. Any other person I knew would have been screaming and carrying on about meeting a vampire. For Dita that was nowhere, in the scale of importance, beside someone, any kind of someone, being in trouble. She'd adjusted to it already. *People respect you*, I'd told her, *because you believe in things*. And it was true, but so rare. Dita had her own beliefs, her own ideas about what mattered. She didn't buy them ready-made.

'The house on Roman Road was a "safe house",' said my mum, taking her mug of sweet coffee. 'Do you know what that is? It's a place where people who are living secret lives can gather and be themselves for a while. You see, there are places all over the world that are *different*, in the same way as we are different from other human beings. They're like cracks or faultlines in the bedrock of normal reality.'

'Oh!' I exclaimed. I'd actually forgotten. 'The night-window!'

She gave me a wry look. 'I thought you must have found it.'

'What window?' demanded Dita.

'It's in the middle bedroom,' I explained. 'I found it the day we went ghost-busting. It doesn't look like a cupboard, it looks like part of the wall. But when you open it, there's a whole coal-sack nebula of darkness inside. A whole other *galaxy*.'

'What?' Dita frowned. 'But I remember that. I was *there*,' she protested. 'I didn't see any coal-sack nebula. It was just an empty cupboard!'

'You can't see the faultlines, Dita,' said my mother. 'You people can't. But you can feel them, whereas we can't. There may be other explanations for ghostly phenomena, but often a "haunted" house, that feels unaccountably eerie and strange, has been built on the site of a fault. We actually feel more comfortable in places of that kind than we do anywhere else, so we tend to use them to meet and socialise. It isn't very sensible. It's not as if we need the weak spots. We're part of the unreal world already. And there are problems. There are fights and wild parties, and there's trouble between us and the inbetweens because of how they feel about the faultlines.' She shook her head. 'Well, I'll explain about that in a moment. Anyway, we use those places. It's stupid, but we do it. Yet another proof that people are all made the same in the end. After a while the house, or whatever kind of site it is, acquires a reputation. The "normal" neighbours start getting too interested in the weird goings-on, and the leaders of the local night-people community decide the clubhouse has to be shut down. That's what happened to the house on Roman Road. It's been abandoned for years.'

'Until my father moved in.'

'Yes. Until Ross came back.'

'But why is he there?' asked Dita. 'I'd have thought he'd have avoided the place.'

My mother shook her head. 'No. He needs to be there. You see, we don't use the faultlines. They have a great fascination, but they're dangerous. We have other ways of travelling through the unreal. But the inbetweens are sure that they would be able to use the faults, and have the freedom of the night-world, if only we would help them. It isn't true, but they all believe it. Ross has something that he thinks is the key to that freedom. He had to take possession of the house, so no one could stop him from getting to the fault.'

She looked from me to Dita. 'You searched the place, didn't you?'

'I'm sorry—' I suddenly remembered that I'd sworn I hadn't been back there.

Mum brushed my apology aside. 'Don't worry. I don't blame you for lying to me. It was my own fault. But did you find anything? I mean, besides the night-window.'

'Yes, we did! We found a strange sort of compass.' Dita tried to describe the contents of the box we'd found under the floor. My mother nodded.

'That's the cloak,' she said. 'That's what he stole. And we have to get it back.'

I didn't see how a metal saucer full of yellow oil could be a 'cloak'.

'But what *is* it?'

She frowned. 'It's hard to explain. It's a kind of second skin, or a shadow; something that is a part of each night-person. Ross thinks that if he could wear it, he would be able to pass through the night-window. He'd be able to fly through time and space, be anywhere, do anything. In a way, he's right. The cloak *is* a gateway between the two worlds. *But not for him.* To one of us, that second skin is like a comfortable garment. On him, on his human body, it would be a shirt of flame that he could not remove. The different kinds of matter reject each other violently. It would be physical, mental, total agony until he died. He knows this is true. He's tried it once, and he was lucky to escape alive. He knows about others – magicians, inbetweens – in the past, who have tried the same thing, and died in agony. But he's convinced there's a secret way to fix the cloak, and that I could help him if I wanted to. So he's kept on following us, trying to wear me down. It's hopeless.'

'Can't you just *take* the thing?' cried Dita. I knew she hated the sound of the word 'hopeless'. 'Now that you know where it is?'

'Did you try to remove the cloak from the box?'

'Well, no . . .'

'You wouldn't have succeeded. Ross is a powerful magician. You would have found it impossible to remove the cloak from the box, or the box from the house.'

Dita insisted, stubbornly. 'I can believe *we* couldn't have done it. But you're so strong, and I know you're not afraid of him. Surely you can bust his spells.'

My mother sighed. 'You've missed the point. The fact that he has it, is not the problem. If I could get it back, he'd just come after us to steal it again. Besides, if I managed to "bust his spells", I'm afraid I would probably destroy the cloak too. Which would be dangerous. It would be like an explosion on the interface between the worlds. I don't know exactly what would happen to the two realities involved, but I don't think we want to find out. No, I can't risk using force. I realised that a long time ago. And Ross will never give up, unless he knows the cloak is permanently out of his reach.'

I was in a daze. This time last week I had known nothing about my own family. I had no background, no past. Suddenly I had a history as strange as some kind of twisted fairytale, and a father. *I have a father*, I kept thinking. *His name is Ross, and he's an evil magician.* Everything that had been wrong with my life was explained. It came back to the disruption between these two and their different kinds of magic. It suddenly made me think of *A Midsummer Night's Dream*, which was a Shakespeare play I'd read, by some accident, in one of the schools I'd passed through. When that story starts, nothing in the natural world can go right because the king and the queen of fairyland, the unreal world, have quarrelled. I thought of me and Mum and Elsa and Max standing outside that house on that dismally cold day, in our scruffy clothes, loaded down with our bags of shopping.

Fairies, skip hence! I have foresworn his bed and company!

Max and Elsa made funny sort of fairies. More like goblins, I thought.

'But you can't go on running and hiding,' Dita burst out. 'You have to fight!'

My mother rolled her empty mug between her palms. 'I

know, you don't have to tell me that.' I noticed she spoke to Dita as if she was another adult, a friend.

'You stopped running,' I said. I understood now what she'd told me a few nights ago. 'You came back here, to where the night-window is. You'd decided to have some sort of confrontation. But why, after all these years? What's changed?'

She looked at me and seemed, again, to be searching for words. 'I'm telling this the wrong way round,' she began at last, abruptly. 'I'd better go back to the beginning. The cloak doesn't belong to me, Andrei, though it was once part of me. It belongs to you. It was born with you. You are, or you could be, like me: a night-person, completely. I wanted you to have the choice, to decide where you wanted to belong. I knew what to do, because my grandmother had told me. I took the cloak from you and kept it . . . like a family heirloom. Ross knew what I'd done. He stole it for himself; he refused to believe that I couldn't help him to use it, and that's when our troubles began.'

She smiled grimly. 'So what's changed? You have, Andrei. You are growing up, and you are changing. You've probably noticed nothing, but I have. Your vision has altered; you need less sleep; you're losing your appetite. Night-people can get by with a lot less light than ordinary humans, and they need to eat less. No ordinary food will harm you, by the way, but you'll find you don't get very hungry. If you pass through the next few months without the cloak, the new differences will fade, and it will be too late for you to choose the night world. You'll still be a *little* different from other people, but no one, not even yourself, will ever need to know it. You've shown no sign of wanting to belong to the night, but you had to have your choice, I owed you that. That's why I had to face up to Ross at last. So I came back here. I knew he'd follow me.'

She pulled a rueful face. 'I took you to the house once, remember? I'd been waiting and nothing had happened. I had to see the house, and I didn't dare leave you three alone and go to it myself. As soon as we got there, I knew I shouldn't have brought you. You and Elsa saw a "ghost", and I realised that Ross had moved in. Then he started his tricks. I was very frightened when I found out that he was threatening you and the children directly. He'd never done that before. But I was determined to hold my ground this time. I had a plan, and Ross was only one of the complications. I had some other awkward people to deal with—'

'I saw them!' I remembered suddenly. 'Those characters I saw you with once by the Monument; you were meeting like secret agents!'

She grinned. 'You kept a close watch on me, didn't you? Yes, those two, and others. They found out that Ross was back, and that he'd set himself up in the old clubhouse. They wanted to settle with him themselves. They don't like inbetweens who make trouble. I've been holding them off. I wanted to handle things my own way. Ross has been nastier than ever, but I've been keeping guard over the children.'

'I saw you,' I whispered.

She laughed faintly. 'Yes, haunting my own house. That was how I discovered things were worse than I'd thought. I knew you had been to Roman Road, and I was worried about that. Then, the night you saw me in the children's room, you thought you saw me jump out of a window. I didn't! I "jumped" back into my own room. Then I heard you running out into the rain. By the time I found you, you were on your way to Roman Road, and you said things that really scared me. I knew he'd somehow broken down your resistance. That's when I decided that my plan was too dangerous. I had to get you away, and think again.'

'Was I in such danger?' I protested. I felt I had to defend my father. 'Okay, he frightened us and he lured me to the house, it's true. But he didn't mean to harm me. He told me he needed my help. I know the puppet-thing was bad, but I don't think he meant it to hurt me. I think he was bluffing, and things went too far—'

She looked at me bleakly. 'Things tend to go to far with Ross. He wants the cloak. For years he's threatened me with all kinds of trouble, to try and make me co-operate. He thinks you can somehow make it over to him, now that you're grown. He also knows that in a few months' time, you'll be no more able to handle the cloak than any other ordinary human being. *This is his last chance.* I don't know how far he'd go to try to *make* you do what he wants. I'm not sure, Andrei. But there was a time when I believed he'd killed Alan.'

I felt the bottom drop out of my stomach.

'Dad died in a car crash. It was an accident.'

'I hope so. But Ross badly wanted him out of the way. That's the trouble with magic, Andrei. It is fuelled by the magic-maker's emotions, and bad emotions make powerful fuel. Anger, greed, hatred, envy . . . If someone loads a gun deliberately, and points it at your head, does it make sense for him to say, "I didn't mean it to go off"? Stop thinking of magic as special. It's the same as any other kind of power, no worse and no better. The same rules apply. And *Ross is dangerous.* You must believe that.'

'Is that why you fell apart after Alan died? Because you thought Ross did it?'

She put down the empty mug and drew herself together, her eyes steady and brave.

'I did fall apart, didn't I. I'm sorry, Andrei. And I'm sorry for the way I've treated you in the last few weeks. When I brought you back here, I was prepared to tell you everything. But as soon as Ross started his games, I started behaving the same way as always. Secrecy and denial . . . I know it doesn't help, but bad habits are hard to break.'

There was a short silence.

'So what are we going to do?' asked Dita softly.

Mum looked at both of us. Some of the happy relief I'd seen, when she confessed the truth about herself and I'd accepted it, was still glowing in her face, and it was good to see. But there was trouble in her eyes.

'I still have my plan, the one I've been working out since I came back here. The Community Fun Day is part of it—'

I exclaimed, 'I *thought* that was odd. You and the Community Fun Day!'

'I had my reasons. My plan needs a public occasion, a time and a place where night-people can mingle easily with humans, and where real magic can be disguised as part of the show. First, we'd have to arrange a parley, a meeting, and let him know our terms. Somebody will have to talk to him. I'm afraid it can't be me.' She sighed. 'We can't talk to each other. It doesn't do any good. But there's no point in that meeting', she went on slowly, 'unless we can go ahead with the rest of the plan.' She looked at me. 'There is a way . . . There's a way to make the cloak safe, and for you and me and Max and Elsa to be free of Ross forever. It all depends on you, Andrei.'

'Me?'

I don't know why I was surprised. I had been listening. I understood the situation. I had come to the moment of choice. Which Andrei was I going to be? I was afraid and bewildered. Part of me felt like yelling No! and running out of the room. I thought of the cloak. I remembered the whorls and gleams in that yellow pool. I remembered the night-window, and my longing. I could almost understand my father's obsession. I thought of being free from fear.

I cleared my throat, which seemed to have become horribly dry.

'What do I have to do?' I said.

Suddenly Dita, who had been kneeling by the coffee tray all this time, stirred and rubbed her arms. 'Before we go any further, could we have a light? No offence, but it's getting a little spooky in here in the pitch dark, listening to you two.'

My mother and I glanced at each other and started to laugh. It was the sweetest sound I'd ever heard: my mother laughing, easy and confident, at a joke we shared.

But that was only for a moment. Dita went to switch on the light.

The room changed. It took on the hard, sharp edges of the daytime world. And my mother began to explain, gravely and gently, just what I had to do to set us free.

Elsa put a spell of protection on me before they sent me out to meet my father. We'd told her everything. We had no choice. She was going to play a vital part in Mum's scheme. She was full of herself, of course. We had to turn the house upside down to find a particular yellow felt-tip that she needed, before she'd do anything. Then she had me up against the wall in the living room, my arms stretched and my legs apart, while she drew around me. I pointed out that the tip of the pen never actually touched the wall, so it didn't matter what colour it was.

'You know nothing,' she told me smugly. 'Now bend down.'

I leant towards her, fuming but patient. She licked her finger, and drew a line of spit down my nose. 'That's it,' she said with a malicious grin. 'You're done.'

I walked out into the sunshine. The spit on my nose itched as it dried, but I had to admit she'd let me off easily. The way things had shaped up in this adventure, I'd have had to do exactly what she told me, no matter what. It was a beautiful June morning. No smog. The sky was like a blue cap, sprayed over with white-gold rays and glowing pink where it fitted neatly onto the rooftops. Every leaf on every hard-working urban tree had a wonderful bright red rim of life around the green. (You can't see that red? I'm sorry for you. But then again, you don't have an evil magician for a daddy.)

People smiled at me as I passed. I thought it was because the sun was shining, or maybe because I was smiling myself – not my usual expression out on the street. As I walked on, and the faces of perfect strangers lit up with beaming affection in front of me, I began to wonder. 'Your mother's a lucky woman,' said an old lady by the bakery. 'You tell her that from me.' I'd never seen this nice old biddy before in my life. Then I caught a glint of yellow on the pavement. I looked down and saw two shining trails, like lines of spider silk, stretching behind me. They reeled away out of sight. I guessed they would lead all the way back to the invisible Andrei-shaped outline on our living room wall.

After Mum had explained everything to her – and Elsa hardly even seemed surprised – I'd cornered my little sister by herself. I'd asked her what she'd *really* known all these years. She said she'd known about the stalker who was following Mum around, and she had a feeling he was a magician, though she hadn't known for sure, until we ran into the litter ghosts. What about her own magic? I asked. Did she know that it was real?

'I knew I was different,' she told me. 'I knew I could do things with my spells. I didn't think about why. It seemed natural to me. I knew that Mum was different too, not like me but in another way. I *wondered* about you, Andrei. You seemed – stuck. If I'd drawn you, I'd have drawn someone shut between two doors, not knowing which one to open.'

I laughed. Elsa! My sister was a kooky character in her own right, magic or no magic. But I had to admit she was pretty smart.

As I passed Agnelli's corner, a bunch of our coolest, moodiest fourth years were mooching down there for an early coffee. I'm not saying these guys were way above me in the pecking order, but I'd been visiting Agnelli's for two solid terms, and none of them had ever deigned to notice my existence before. Usually they stepped round me as if I was a dog's mess. Today, they stopped and smiled. The Mighty Manaj tossed back his raven-black movie-star locks and called: 'Hey, Andrei. Nice to meet you.'

I had put a note through the door of the haunted house, explaining our offer. I'd asked my father to meet me outside *Occasions*, the card shop, this Saturday at noon. It was a few minutes to twelve by the library clock when I arrived there, and the whole High Street was awash with feel-good-for-Andrei. I kept expecting people to burst into song. He was on time. There was nothing unusual about his appearance – a thin man of average height, about forty, in a shabby tweed sports jacket and clean faded jeans. He was wearing a roll-neck jumper; you couldn't see the scars. You'd have taken him for a teacher or something.

'Hello, Andrei.'

He looked at the pavement at my feet. 'I see you brought some insurance. Your little sister fixed you up, right?'

I shrugged. 'I think she laid it on a bit thick, actually.'

My father wasn't smiling. He seemed to be immune to the feel-good effect.

'So, Milada sent you to talk. Where do you want to go?'

I took him to McDonalds. It was still early for lunchtime and the place wasn't crowded. I felt very odd. I'd heard about this kind of meeting. It was exactly what you do with an estranged father. You meet them for one day a month. They take you to McDonalds, and you sit there with them, awkwardly making conversation. And this was my father. He didn't offer to buy me anything. I bought myself a large chocolate shake, and he acquired a cup of black coffee. Somehow (I was watching carefully, but I don't know how) he did not pay for it.

We took our things and went to sit down. At least we had something to talk about.

'So,' he said slowly. 'So that's it, that's why she came

back. She's decided to surrender, after all these years. Why? Why should I trust you?'

I looked for myself in his face. His eyes were dark hazel, like mine, but I couldn't tell if he looked like me. There was so much I wanted to ask him: about his life, his past, his own childhood. Did he remember me at all? How had he been living all these years? I could see it would be no good. He was staring back at me intently. But he wasn't interested in our family likeness. I could tell he was trying desperately to gauge whether our offer was genuine. It was the cloak, and only the cloak. This man was so *hungry* it was a disease. It was as if he was in really bad pain and couldn't concentrate on a single other idea. You'd be wasting your time trying to talk to someone like that about anything except painkillers.

'I think she's tired of running.' I answered. 'And there's me.'

'You?' He gripped the cup, so that it crumpled and scalding hot coffee boiled out over his hand. He didn't seem to notice. 'What about you?'

'She wants me to have a normal life. She wants us to be finished with you, so I can stay in one school, take my exams and all that. And there's Max and Elsa too, of course.'

'Mmm. Is that so?' He looked down vaguely at his hand, and wiped it on his sleeve. 'It's not like her to give up. She's the stubbornest woman alive. All those years, she told me what I wanted was impossible. Why should I trust her now?'

'Look,' I said, my voice rising helplessly. '*I don't know.* This is completely strange to me, I can hardly believe what's been happening. She says you can have "the cloak", whatever that means. She says I have to do something, some kind of hocus-pocus, to help you take control of this thing. She says that's what you want, and when it's done you'll leave us alone. I don't know you. I only know you're my father, because Mum says you are. I just want to get on with my life. I want things to be normal and ordinary again. So does she. I mean, as far as we *can* be normal. And we'll agree to whatever it takes—'

I couldn't have faked the feeling in that speech. I was telling the truth, the absolute truth. He must believe it. He stared at me for another long moment, and I trembled.

'She hasn't told you anything,' he said softly. 'Not a thing.'

He smiled bitterly, remembering. 'That's Milada. That's like her. She would never tell me. Time and again I begged her to be reasonable. I wasn't asking much, just a little co-operation from my own woman. But she wouldn't give in. She kept on saying I was asking the impossible. I did everything I could to try and make her see sense but no, not Mili. She would not give in . . .'

I could see that he was ready to go on like this indefinitely, telling over his troubles and chewing over his anger. But he had relaxed. He'd made up his mind.

'Okay, suppose I go along with this. How do we do it?'

I put an envelope on the table and pushed it across to him. He picked it up, watching my face all the time, and opened it. It wasn't sealed. I watched as he unfolded the Fun Day prize draw programme. He read the whole thing carefully, from the list of raffle prizes to the local advertisments on the back. Taped inside there was a purple printed ticket for one visit to Milada's Magic Hall of Mirrors. He took it out, held it between his finger and thumb and sort of sniffed at it. He was checking it for magic, I guessed.

'Fancy printing,' he remarked.

'It's cheap these days.'

I sucked loudly on my chocolate shake, in bravado.

'The programme will get you into the Fun Day enclosure. All you have to do is come to the "Hall of Mirrors" tent at four in the afternoon, and bring the cloak with you. That's where we'll do the handover. But you come unarmed. No puppets.'

He folded his ticket inside the programme and slipped them both into an inside pocket of his jacket. He sat back, took a gulp of his coffee and set the cup down.

'Max and Elsa,' he remarked, 'they're nice-looking kids.'

He had called me a 'nice-looking kid' when he met me in the haunted house, just before he turned his ectoplasm-powered monster loose on me. I didn't think it was a well-omened compliment.

'It'd be a shame if anything happened to them.' His voice was still pleasant, but there was a cold threat in his eyes. 'I mean, something more than a Hallowe'en practical joke. Something nasty. You hear about that sort of thing too often these days. A child disappears, snatched in a moment. And then there's the police search, the tv appeals, and the horrible long wait . . . until you hear the really bad news.'

I looked down and sucked some more of my shake. I wouldn't answer him.

'I'm going to trust you, Andrei, you and your mother. I'm going to accept your offer. But you think about what I've said about the children. Tell her to think about it too. And don't try anything stupid.'

I suppose he might have worked out some more original lines if his brain hadn't been full of the cloak. He glanced round with an expression of deep contempt for the place and the people, mixed with a kind of wonder. He was like a prisoner who could hardly believe he was going to escape at last.

'An ordinary life!' He laughed. 'Is that what you want? You can keep it, Andrei.'

I heard his chair scrape on the floor. I looked up and saw him walking out of the door. There was nothing that would tell you he'd just threatened to kidnap two small children and do them some terrible harm. No one in McDonalds could feel the hunger that was eating him up; no one knew about his magical powers. He was a thin man with sour eyes. No one gave him a second glance. It may seem strange, but I pitied him. I sat there for about ten minutes, while the lunchtime bustle built up around me. Elsa's feel-good effect had switched off. I had lost my glow. A waitress came to wipe up Ross's spilled coffee and gave me a nasty look. I went home to tell the other conspirators that everything was going as planned.

Seven

*I*T WAS ABOUT HALF-PAST TWO ON FUN DAY AFTERNOON. I'd eaten – or rather, I'd nibbled the corners from a plate of corned beef hash and baked beans – in the stewards' tent, in a bedlam of chatter (vegetarian option: sunflower seed lasagne). I'd been gophering all morning as one of the unskilled general assistants on the Fun Day crew, and I hadn't managed to get away to lunch before two. I stuffed my paper plate in the bin and walked out, being careful not to catch the eye of anyone who might need a gopher. I'd done my stint. I had other business now.

We'd been afraid all week that the fine weather might break. It looked as if we were safe. The sky was blue, and though the temperature wasn't exactly tropical, it was not bad for an English June. The bunting I'd helped to mend rattled cheerfully in the sunshine, and the trees round the edge of the enclosure glowed with life. The St George Mummers and Morris Men were striding about in costume, in search of an audience. A woman in the Co-op Bank tent was pinning up something exciting about fixed price mortgages, on a poster board. The traditional British Table Sale was gearing up to do a roaring trade in dodgy 'house clearance' items, away beyond the beer tent. The punters were streaming in, examining their lucky number programmes and spreading out to wander from stall to stall.

I stood and watched the Sumo Wrestler Arena, where kids were paying to be inserted into huge, pillow-like padded suits, in which they floundered around hilariously, trying to fight with each other. Next to their pitch was the

Velcro Wall, where smaller children were being dressed up in velcro overalls and flung bodily at a three-metre tower which was also covered in velcro, so that they stuck to it like burrs. At the Kathakali dance stage, a fat man in pleated white skirts was lying flat on his back on the boards, having his face painted green by Des Mukarjee, Dita's father. He was dressed in white linen too, naked to the waist and looking distinctly parky. Mrs Mukarjee, in her best sari, was watching from the crowd, holding a woolly jacket in her arms.

'He could wear his cardigan!' she said to me. 'For heaven's sake, no one would mind if he wore a cardigan. Why are all my family so stubborn?' She was the narrator who would explain what was supposed to be going on when the dance-drama began. I could tell that she had stage fright. She wanted to chat to someone, to get her through the awful wait until her performance began. I knew the feeling! But I couldn't help her. I passed on.

I stopped beside the coconut shy, where boys and young men – and some girls – were lining up for the age-old trial of prowess. I was thinking it was strange to see such an ancient attraction still going alongside the Velcro Wall and the Sumo wrestlers. The coconut shy man was beside me, a cheery-looking old fellow in an unlikely costume that consisted of a baggy Guns & Roses sweatshirt and a pair of black tracksuit bottoms so old they'd turned green. He grinned and winked.

'You'd be surprised. I go round all the fêtes and fairs, and some days I make twice on this what I do on the Velcro. There's no game like an old game.'

I jumped. I didn't know I'd been thinking aloud.

He gave me a sly glance. 'No game like an old game, eh, Andrei?' He took a handful of misshapen wooden balls from the box at his feet. 'Try your luck, young man?'

'No thanks. Coconuts are cheaper in the market.'

'You know that and I know that. But the punters have a

different mentality, and that's how we make our living.' He put his free hand on my arm. His eyes glinted strangely.

'Remember me to your ma. Say, the coconut shy man wishes her luck. She knows.'

I moved on. My arm was tingling where he'd touched me.

By the beer tent, I saw the little fat bag-lady I'd seen once by the Monument in her bundle of shawls. She looked round and caught me staring at her. For an instant, then, she was outlined in a swirl of darkness, like dark and shining wings uplifted. Then she'd vanished into the crowd. I started looking for the tall, thin white man. I didn't spot him, but there were other faces that looked out at me and seemed to know me, eyes that gleamed when they caught mine, ordinary-looking people who were not ordinary at all. Whatever happened this afternoon, we weren't alone, Mum and Dita and Elsa and I. The night-people were here in force.

Finally, I headed for the Hall of Mirrors. Our board said 'Open at 3'. There was a small crowd outside. I unhitched the rope in the entrance and slipped inside. The Hall of Mirrors was built of moveable panels covered in reflective foil, arranged in a maze of narrow passageways. Some of the panels were convex or concave, to do the usual distorting tricks. But most of the fun was in the illusion of never-ending passages, the impossible vistas, the places where you met yourself or thought you were falling, or climbing – or found a mirror that reflected something completely different from what was in front of it. Nothing was real. It was all done with lights and clever angles. In the centre of the maze there was a tiny cubicle where – if everything worked – you would meet your own ghost, see yourself become invisible, and then speedily be funnelled out of the tent to make way for the next adventurer.

My mother was on a stepladder, doing something to the wiring that festooned the canvas roof (concealed from the customers, more or less, by lots of flame-resistant silver streamers). She was calling instructions to Celie, who was at the control desk below. Dita and Elsa were watching.

'Try the red switch,' called my mother. 'Now move the two *green* knobs—'

A gossamer flickering flowed through the tent, like aurora borealis in miniature.

'Now the other ones, in the middle. Move them half way—'

I stared up at my mother, perched on her ladder, a row of screwdrivers in her back pocket and a roll of gaffer tape slung on her wrist. I was amazed at her competence. She sounded so confident. My mother, my hopeless neurotic mother, could be like this all the time, I thought. She could have a proper job, go out to work and go out to play . . .

All those years, ever since I was born, she'd given up so much. She had given up her night-people powers so that Max and Elsa and I – especially me – could have a normal life. She'd protected us from Ross. That first night, when she'd told me her story, I'd been too astonished to think of her life. It was only later that I began to understand how trapped she'd been, between her own secret nature and Ross's demands. No wonder she'd been a neurotic wreck sometimes. But she'd never given up, never. And now at last she could be free in the daytime and in the night-world too. I was so dazzled by this idea that for a moment I forgot the horror of what had to be done first.

She glanced round and saw me.

'That's it, Celie. I think we're ready for those punters.' She came briskly down.

'Well?' she said.

'There's quite a crowd,' I answered. 'I saw plenty of your old friends.'

My mother nodded. Celie looked puzzled – as well she might, since Mum wasn't supposed to have any 'old friends'. Mum turned to her. 'It's nearly three. Can you hang on here and keep the public out, while I have a couple of minutes with my staff?'

We left Celie guarding the door, and Mum and Dita and Elsa and I retired – using a secret short cut – to the centre of the maze. The little cubicle was floored in glistening plastic, and empty except for a canvas and metal director's chair, that was reflected in infinite regress in the mirror walls. Under Mum's present lighting everything seemed liquid blue, even the air. I was surprised that bubbles didn't come out of our mouths when we talked.

'Does everyone know what to do?' said Mum. 'Elsa, are you ready?'

Elsa nodded, looking serious and a little bit frightened.

'Dita,' Mum went on, 'you're going to be on the door. All you have to do is take the money and let people through. When Andrei comes back, with *him*, you let them through. Then you say there's a temporary fault, and don't let anyone else in. If everything works out, it won't be for long. I'll come and tell you when it's all right to let the public in again. If I don't come after about twenty minutes, and there are people waiting, then you close up shop permanently and tell them to go away. Use your judgement, Dita. You won't need to fetch help. If something's gone badly wrong, my "old friends" will know and they'll come to you.'

'I think I'd better go,' I said. 'I ought to be at the gate.'

Dita and I went out. Celie was in a hurry to get back to her own show and didn't ask us what we'd been up to. Dita sat down at the cash table. She took off her watch and handed it to me. 'You'll need this.'

I was used to managing without one, but I appreciated the gesture.

'Of course. Thanks.'

We exchanged a last glance. I wondered if I looked as tense and big-eyed as she did. 'Good luck,' she muttered. 'See you on the other side . . .'

I unhooked the rope for her. The queue surged forward. I walked away, hands stuffed in my pockets. My right hand held the watch, my left was closed tightly around the little stone figure of Ganesh, my luck charm. Hindu divinities were meant to work for humans, I supposed, not my people. But maybe he'd stretch a point for Dita's sake. I certainly needed all the help I could get.

I mingled in the crowd by the entrance gate. There was a country dance set going on, on the music stage. I could hear the caller yelling out instructions, and the sparky, insistent beat of that old-time native music, peppered by the thump of galloping feet. The Barn Dance team would be followed, I knew, by Domina Du, an aspiring female rap duo from my school; and then a New Country showband from the Irish pub; and then there'd be a set from the Likrish Alsorts, our local teen-idols. This mish-mash was the committee's idea of equal opportunities airtime. The punters were going to be seasick by the time the raffle was drawn. For something to do, I bought myself a cream cheese and tandoori prawn jacket potato. It was a revolting combination. But where was Ross? Would he really come? I thought over what Mum had said, that night in her bedroom, when she was explaining the plan.

'Ross keeps the cloak well pinned down. It can't be taken from him without violence: I've found out that much over the years. We have to get him to bring it to us, and take off the spells that bind it, of his own accord. We're going to tell him that I'm finally ready to admit there *is* a way to make the cloak safe, and I'm prepared to fix it and hand it over to him. I'm going to insist that this handover happens in a public place, for his protection and our own. He's to bring the cloak to my magic show, on the Fun Day . . .'

I held the potato confection in one hand and pulled out Dita's watch. It had stopped, of course. I shoved up to the gate, where Mr Archer the butcher was taking money and handing out programmes. He looked up at me, shaking his head.

'It was supposed to be mint yoghurt.'

'What?'

'On the tandoori. I saw you bought one. Terrible muddle with the ordering. Terrible muddles all over.'

'Mr Archer, what time is it?' I demanded.

He glanced at his wrist. 'Just gone four. I'm supposed to be off here. I don't know where my replacement's got to. I can't stay. Andrei, you'll have to go and tell—'

But my father was suddenly there, his shoulders hunched in the cold sunlight. He showed Mr Archer his programme; our eyes met.

I think I left my potato on the cash table. I don't remember. I only know I found myself walking with the magician through the Fun Day crowds. The Barn Dance accordion and fiddle wailed and thumped over the PA. The mummers were having an earnest confab by the beer tent. St George, his arms in painted armour folded over his impressive gut, was demanding bitterly: *'So, where IS the Green Man, at this point in time and space?'*

I led my father to the Hall of Mirrors, everything zinging in my ears.

'You're holding something back, Andrei.'

'Me?'

He eyed me up and down. He was thin and hungry as a stray dog, a vicious dog that would bite you while it snatched the food you offered it. There was an oblong bulge in the front of his sports jacket. That must be the box, the sheeny-pale box that we'd found under the floor in the empty house. He kept one arm tightly pressed against it.

'You. Don't be stupid, Andrei. This isn't magic. I don't need magic to tell me you are sweating, and it's because there's something you don't want me to know. You'd better tell me or I'm leaving. Don't mess me around. Think of the kids. *Think* about them, Andrei.'

I swallowed hard and rubbed my sweaty hands on my jacket.

'I don't know what you mean. I'm scared, that's all. I don't *like* this. I'm sure there's stuff Mum isn't telling me. Can you explain, Dad? What's the deal? What's going to happen to me when I do this – this disgusting magic thing with Elsa?'

This was the way we played him. We knew he was bound to be suspicious. He'd swallow the hook, but then he'd start to fight back. So we had to make him feel that *we* were more afraid and anxious than he was.

Ross listened, and finally smiled that secretive smile. 'Nothing,' he told me. 'Nothing at all, Andrei. You won't feel a thing.'

He ran the tip of his tongue over his lips, and scratched the crisp black beard along his jaw. 'Your sister's a talented little girl. You know, I've suspected for a year or two that you had a junior magician in the family. This time, when we all moved back here, I knew. Well, well, lucky little Elsa. You know, there's a lot I could teach her.'

'She doesn't want anything to do with you,' I said quickly. 'You're to leave her alone. Mum says you'll go away and leave us in peace after this.'

'I swear I will,' he told me solemnly. 'If your mother makes the cloak safe for me, I swear you won't ever hear from me again.' But his eyes flickered. The thought of stealing Elsa away was obviously attractive. 'What d'you think I'm going to do?' he demanded virtuously. 'Kidnap the child?'

He was forgetting that he'd threatened to do just that when we last met.

'Right,' I said, nervously. 'Right. Of course not.'

'I can't take her away if she doesn't want to come. I

wouldn't do that. But if she wants to, later, does anyone have a right to stop her from seeing me? I don't think so.'

'No. No, of course not . . .'

We had arrived at the tent. Business looked good. There was a line of people waiting in ones and twos. The afternoon was fiercely bright but the breeze was getting colder. We moved up to the front of the queue, not speaking. Maybe he was planning how he'd make Elsa his apprentice to spite Mum. When he reached the front, he took out his complimentary ticket. He looked at Dita and looked at me and his eyes narrowed.

'It's the ticket, isn't it?' he burst out, sharply and suddenly. 'I know there's still something wrong. It's not that guff about me running off with your sister. It must be this.'

He tore up the scrap of purple card and tossed the pieces in the air. The people behind us were getting interested. 'I think you'll find I'm on the guest list,' said my father. He dived past Dita, unhooked the rope for himself, and strode into the maze.

Dita replaced the rope. 'I'm sorry,' she announced. 'We have a small problem. We're going to have to take a break. It'll be a few minutes.'

She turned our board around. On the back, amid purple stars, it said OUT TO LUNCH. BACK SOON.

'Goodbye,' she said to me. She gave a quick little grin and changed that. 'I mean, good luck, Andrei.'

I went round to the exit where the punters were funnelled out. I lifted the canvas wall and slipped inside. The space between the skin of the tent and the panels of the maze was green and gloomy. It smelled of bruised grass. I unhooked the fastening between two panels and squeezed myself between them. In the centre of the maze, my mother was standing against the wall in her white teeshirt and scruffy jeans. (She didn't need to dress up for the show. She didn't appear in it, she just managed the effects.) Her arms were folded, her face was set and drawn. She looked exactly as you'd expect someone to look, who had been defeated at last, and was forced to submit to somebody she hated. Ross stood opposite, hands in his pockets. Elsa was sitting in the director's chair. I glanced at my father, who grinned at me jauntily, and went over to Elsa.

'Now you're going to do your trick, Elsa,' said Mum gently. 'Do what I told you; concentrate and don't rush.'

She came and stood behind the chair, her hands resting lightly on Elsa's shoulders. I stood in front, holding Elsa's hands. They felt hot, small and dry. Elsa frowned. I didn't feel anything more than that, for a moment. Then suddenly there was something warm, running like melted wax. It was coming from me, Elsa was pulling somehow, so it went running and oozing between our fingers. My mother shuddered as if someone was dropping ice down her back. I saw her bite her lip.

'Does it hurt?' whispered Elsa, in a small voice unlike her usual bossy tone.

'No,' I said. 'Go on. Just do it.'

At last she let go. There was something insubstantial glistening on her fingers; it was hard to see in the blue light. She brought her palms together . . . with a kneading sort of gesture that I recognised. It was horrible to watch, especially since Elsa, doing this trick, was repeated all over the mirror walls. '*I hate this* . . .' I muttered, which was no word of a lie.

Elsa opened her hands. She was holding a small pinkish blob, like a lump of bubblegum. 'I've done it,' she whispered, sounding scared. 'Mummy, I feel sick.'

My mother took the bolus of ectoplasm. 'Thank you, Elsa, my brave girl. Now don't be afraid, but in a moment you're going to feel *very* tired.' She looked stern. 'And you are not to do that again. Do you hear me? Not for any reason, at least not until you're grown up; and not then if you've any sense. There are other kinds of magic, safer and better spells—'

'Mummy!' protested Elsa, reproachfully. All the blood had drained out of her pointy little face.

'Oh baby, I'm sorry,' cried Mum. 'It's my nerves. I get bossy when I'm worried; I can't help it.' She helped Elsa out of the chair. 'Go and curl up on our coats in the back of the tent. I'll bring you some hot sweet tea in a moment.'

'*I hate tea*,' muttered Elsa, and trailed off down the punters' exit funnel, looking rather pathetic. My sister, the great magician.

My mother stared after her. I knew how she'd hated having to get Elsa to do that. For years she had protected her children. She'd kept us from harm and she'd kept her trouble and secrets hidden as best she could, at whatever cost to herself. But for today we had needed a magic show that would convince my father, so she'd been forced to put Elsa's power to use. Ross should be satisfied. He had finally managed to get past my mother's defences, after all.

He had watched all this without a word. I didn't know how he'd been reacting, because I hadn't dared to look his way. Now he ambled across and took Elsa's place in the director's chair. My mother held out the bolus of ectoplasm.

'Here it is,' she told him. 'Essence of Andrei. There's enough of the night-world in this lump to protect you through the bonding. After that, the cloak will be part of you. He's going through the change; that's why this is possible. It's the only time the switch could work.'

Ross glanced at me uneasily. 'Hey. Does he understand what you're saying?'

'I understand enough,' I said sourly. 'I never wanted the "cloak". I wish I'd never heard of it, or any of this "night-world" stuff.'

He grinned in triumph, holding the thing like a bubble-gum ball in his cupped hand. 'We always knew,' he murmured. 'We always *knew* there was a way, and you full-bloods were holding out on us.' Then he heaved a deep sigh of satisfaction. 'Yeah,' he said softly. 'It's true. You've given in. I've won. Poor Mili.'

'Get on with it.' she muttered, refusing to raise her eyes. 'You'd better hurry. The stuff has to be fresh.'

Still holding the bolus in one hand, he slid the box of smooth pale wood out of his jacket and laid it on his knees. I could see his hands shaking, between fear and longing. He tipped back his head and chucked the ectoplasm down his throat. I saw him swallow, and then he caught my eye.

'Why are *you* still here? You want to watch?'

'Yes—' I breathed.

He gave me an impatient stare, but made no further protest. He sat with his eyes intent, as if he was studying the inner effect of the dose he'd just swallowed.

'Are you going to be all day?' muttered my mother.

He laughed. Then he opened the box. None of the contents had shifted while he was carrying it around. The compass needle lay on the wax of the night-light thing. The yellow oily liquid glistened. He touched the needle with one fingertip. There was a visible crackle of discharge, and a sound like someone snapping a twig. He carefully lifted out the night-light and needle together, and set them down on the blue reflecting floor.

He looked up at my mother and chuckled. 'Free at last, eh?'

Then he put the fingertips of both hands into the yellow, oily stuff in the saucer . . . and drew out a yellow veil, a golden veil. The yellow and the gold turned midnight hole-in-the-world black as the cloak hit the air, but kept their brightness. It was like a skein of dark that had a million stars melted into it. It was a thing, a place, a path to the other side of things, where dark and light are *not different* from each other, the way they are in this solid world.

And it was reflected a thousand on a thousand times in the mirrors.

I heard my father breathing. Three ragged breaths, and then he whispered to himself *do it* . . . For a moment he vanished into night. I knew he'd lifted the cloak of shadow over his head, and he was wrapping it around his shoulders. The melted-stars darkness spiralled around, unwove itself from the fabric of the air . . . and it was gone.

He reappeared. He was sitting very upright, his mouth slightly open, his eyes wide. 'It worked. It's mine. It's a part of me!'

He crowed in triumph. 'I knew I'd win, Mili. I knew I'd beat you down in the end.'

She wouldn't look at him. She was staring at the floor.

My father began to laugh uproariously. I started to think Mum must have made a mistake. He had the cloak and he wasn't suffering. Now he had all the power, and we were at his mercy. Leave us in peace! I knew there was no chance of that.

He stretched his arms and jumped to his feet, still laughing.

'Come on, Mili. Don't be a sore loser! We're equals now. You know, as far as I'm concerned, you've always been my wife. You're still my wife—'

She lifted her head then, and looked at him.

He knew he'd been tricked before the pain began. I saw him realising it. I saw him read the shame and pity in her eyes, I saw him guess the truth. Then the pain flared up, twisting his face like fire twisting a scrap of paper . . . and he began to scream.

He stumbled around and half fell into the exit funnel. We heard the screaming die into a thin, animal keening sound as he ran out of the tent, into the June sunlight and the crowds.

My mother's breath came in hard gasps. But she

stopped herself from crying. She rubbed her eyes with her fingers. 'Go on!' she said harshly. 'Go after him. Finish it!'

Elsa lay curled up on a pile of coats already asleep. I rushed past her. Outside, the night-people must have been waiting. There was nothing shocking to be seen. There was no figure writhing in the grass, moaning like a damned soul. Some friends – one of them was the man from the coconut shy – were apparently dealing with a drunken mate of theirs. The drunk was shouting and flailing his arms about, but he seemed to be in good hands. There was laughter as he passed through the crowds, and the way the other men helped him along looked kindly, though they moved at a surprising rate.

I lost them somehow. I ran, falling over little kids with balloons, stumbling through roped-off pitches. The Barn Dance was still going, or maybe it was their second set. The music ran through my brain, making me feel as if I was caught up in a country dance myself, a moving pattern that made sense to the other people involved but not to me. Two children, stuffed inside those comic beached-whale Sumo Wrestler suits, were trying hard to fall on top of each other while the folk around them whooped and cackled. I stumbled into the arena, picked myself up and scrambled out again. In the distance, the drunk's friends were propping him against a tree on the edge of the Common. The coconut shy man – I saw his skinny figure dark against the virulent light – was making strange, priestly gestures over the body.

'Leave him alone!' I yelled. 'He's mine!'

I ran like mad, but the crowd kept getting in my way. When I reached the spot, they'd all vanished. There was nothing by the tree but a can of strong lager, rolling on its side. The air was full of the rank, sweet smell of the drink. The coconut man must have been sprinkling it about.

They'd left him here, where he could scream and rave, and passers by would smell the drink and take no notice. But my father was gone.

I crossed the road and jogged on. The High Street felt strangely empty. It was teatime on a Saturday afternoon, and too cold for the hopeful pavement tables outside the Hunnypot Tearoom. It was time for everyone who wasn't having fun on the Common, to nip home and catch the sports results. The breeze had become a cold wind, whipping up scraps of litter. I saw a crumpled human shape propped against the wall in the supermarket loading bay. But it was only old Carlsberg Special.

'Have you seen anyone?' I yelled. 'He might have been acting drunk, he might have been making a row. Have you seen anyone like that go by?'

Old Carlsberg shook his matted head.

'He wasn't drunk, lad. It was the horrors. I've been that way myself. You get these . . . things, crawling on you. Some kind of red lice, big as crayfish.' He plucked at the front of his coat. 'You can get something for it from the doctors. But it's not the drink that does it! It's only when you can't *get* a drink. I've never had the horrors from drink. D'you believe that?'

'Yes,' I gasped. 'Absolutely. Where did he go?'

'I dunno. Off somewhere. Is he a friend of yours?'

'He's my father.'

I had to walk, because I didn't know how far he'd get. I had to look into every doorway and peer down every alley. I had Dita's watch, but since it had stopped before four, I don't know how long it took me to reach the house on Roman Road. I don't suppose it mattered to my father. There's no time in hell.

I found him in the middle bedroom. He was lying face downward on the floor, his arms reaching out to the window-panel. He didn't move when I came in. He looked as rigid as if he had been cut out of cardboard. I don't know what anyone else would have seen, but to my perception his body was outlined in flickering darkness. I knew what I had to do. I knelt beside him on the dusty boards. I lifted from him the shirt of flame, my birthright cloak of shadow, and put it on myself. For a split second (there isn't any time in hell, but I was just visiting, so I didn't get the full effect) I felt the incredible, unbelievable pain of helpless revulsion that had been tearing through every molecule of his agonised body. Then the night skin sank into the fabric of Andrei. It became a part of me, the way it was supposed to be, and passed forever out of my father's reach.

He rolled over on his back, and lay there staring at the ceiling. All the skin that I could see – his face and throat and hands – was a livid, bruised purple, as if he'd been caught and crushed nearly to death by some kind of complex machinery. The old scars from the last time he'd tried on the cloak stood out darker still.

'I'm sorry,' I said. 'You were right to be suspicious; we were lying. The trick was, that there isn't any trick. There's no way you can have the cloak. D'you believe that now?'

He sat up very carefully, feeling himself and looking down in dread, as if he expected to find several bones broken and his entrails in a heap on the floor.

'Yeah, I believe it. Thank you for the gentle lesson.' He shook his head, very carefully and slowly. 'I just can't believe I was taken in like that. You swore you didn't want the thing, Andrei.'

'You see, she had to wait until I was old enough to make up my mind. She believed it had to be my own decision, which world I would belong to. I didn't say a word that wasn't true, Ross. I didn't *want* to be different.'

We had to get him to take his spells off the cloak. But Mum knew that if he did that, he'd want to put it on straight away. He'd believe that she had fixed things, because he wanted *badly* to believe that. But he wouldn't give us any chance of changing our minds. So that was how it had to be done. We'd had to let him put it on, and then I was the only one who could take it from him. There was no other solution in the end. It wasn't only for our own sakes. If he gave up hope, when he knew I was too old to 'help' him, he might have tried to destroy the cloak on purpose, and disrupted the fabric of two realities. We couldn't risk that. This was the only way we could make the cloak safe forever. It had to become mine.

'It was about time for the last round of the fight,' muttered Ross. 'The last round. Dooing! And I'm out for the count.'

He stared at me. I didn't feel anything. My transformation scene was a non-event for me, so far. But not to him. To him it was the end of the road, the final *no*. I saw all that ruthless longing and plotting, the whole purpose of his life, crumpling up inside him like a runaway train hitting the buffers. And the thing he had wanted so badly was mine as easily as if I'd picked up an old jacket of my mother's and slung it round my shoulders. I shouldn't have been sorry. He'd stolen my birthright, betrayed my mother's trust, harassed us for years, and maybe that wasn't the worst he'd done. I shouldn't have been sorry, but I was.

I had a sense – it was like looking down a cliff of years – of how his hunger for the powers of the night had eaten him away inside, until there was nothing left of the love he'd once had for my mother, or any feeling he might have had for me.

It's hard to give up entirely on your own father. I didn't leave straight away, that evening. We sat and talked for a little while in the empty room. I can't remember much of what we said. I know he tried to explain away the bad things. He admitted he'd threatened and persecuted us, but he swore he didn't 'really mean any harm'. Don't worry, I wasn't fooled. But you can understand someone, and forgive them, without having to say they never did anything wrong. Without even thinking they won't do wrong again. The way I see it, he's a lot like me – obsessive about what he wants from life, and determined not to change his ideas – and he let those traits carry him along too far. I've thought about that, and I have taken the warning.

I think he'll never be able to handle being with Mum. She's poison to him, like heroin or alcohol to a reformed addict. She doesn't hate him or anything, but it's completely over for her, and that's what he'll never be able to accept. *Giving up* is something my father and I find very difficult. We tend to hang on, long after it makes no sense. So there'll be no family reunion. But I'll see him again, I suspect. He'll turn up from time to time.

Anyway, we talked, while the cold summer evening grew colder and my night-vision sharpened to a pitch I'd never known before. It was strange indeed to be in that house and see what could be seen there when the distracting daylight was gone. I didn't say anything to my father, but I suppose he guessed what was happening. Eventually he said he had to pack, he wanted to be on his way. He didn't invite me down to his lair in the basement. So I said goodbye and went home.

I let myself in and went straight upstairs. I sat down on the stool in front of her pine chest and looked into the mirrors that stood on top of it. All my life, as far back as I could remember, I had told myself that I longed for just one thing: to be ordinary and normal, to have a routine life, to be like everybody else. My mother knew how I felt. That was why it was so difficult for her to tell me the truth. But when there was only one way for us to escape from my father's obsession, when I had no choice . . . then I knew what I really wanted. I don't think there are many 'free' choices in real life. We like to think we're choosing, but really we are running, like water, into the path of our own innermost nature. I looked in the mirror. It wasn't like the Dracula movies, where the monster has no reflection. I saw something all right. I saw the shadow, the opposite of real. I can't describe it better than that. But it was me. Me to the depths of me. It explained a lot. It felt right. I won't say more.

Eight

I NEVER WENT BACK TO THE HOUSE OF NIGHT. IT BURNED down in the early hours of the Sunday morning after the Community Fun Day. We heard the bells and sirens and saw the glow in the sky from our bedroom windows. My mother had been expecting it. At about ten o'clock that night, a while after I got back from Roman Road, she'd had a phone call. She didn't tell us who called her or what they said (old habits die hard). When the fire started, though, she wasn't surprised. She said, *Don't worry Andrei. They let your father clear out first.* There'd always be someone else like Ross, helplessly drawn to the faultline and causing aggravation. The night-people had decided to take action.

The fire removed number 2121 Roman Road as neatly as if it had been snipped out by a pair of scissors. It fried the place, house and garden, right down to bare earth. The report in our local freesheet said the Fire Service officers were amazed that so much heat had been generated, and yet the fire hadn't spread to any other property. Arson was suspected, possibly in connection with goods that were found stored in the ex-off-licence next door. Apparently it had mostly been cartons of cigarettes, and they were probably stolen. But nothing was ever proved.

I meant to go and look at the site. But for the first few days I was slightly afraid to be seen loitering there, and then as time went by, taken up in other things. It was a quiet day in October when I finally went back to Roman Road.

The sky was low and even the rat-track traffic seemed

half asleep. The gateposts were still standing, alone in front of a patch of blackened rubble. The hazard-tape that had been left around the site by the Fire Service had been pulled down by kids or blown away by the wind. Orange and white scraps of it clung to the stakes that remained.

Now that I knew the truth. I could make out the word beginning with REF that had once been carved on the lefthand stone: *Refugio Noctis* – refuge for the night, a shelter from the storm. But the refuge had been polluted and the shelter had been broken down, and now there was nothing left but ashes and emptiness.

I picked my way through the ghost of a house into what had been the garden – though you could tell no difference, the fire had burned so fiercely. I climbed into a square pit in the ground that must once have been the sunken room. I remembered the day we went ghost-busting, Dita and Elsa and I; and the rich and rare strangeness we had found. My mother had told me that she believed the murals were genuine, and Elsa was right, there had been a temple here two thousand years ago. Or so she'd been told by the night-people who had used the clubhouse. The Roman settlers, and the British before them, had known that this was an uncanny place, and they had paid their respects to a god whose name they did not know.

It was in the sunken room that Dita had felt the strangeness most strongly, though to me the 'faultline' was a pit of darkness hidden in an upstairs cupboard. My mother said flaws in reality were like that. They had a peculiar relation to normal space. Dimensions were folded around each other – or something like that.

I wished we'd spent more time exploring. I wished I'd found out more.

The locus, the faultline, was still there. It could reassert itself eventually, Mum said, and there'd be a haunted house again. Or a haunted office block. Or a haunted empty lot, if the site was left derelict. But not for a while.

I stood in the ashes, looking up at the indigo sky. This place was like me, I thought. Something had ended here, and something else had not yet begun. I stretched out my arms in front of me, and saw the flickering corona of darkness that outlined them. I had wanted to be normal . . . but to belong to the night was *normal* to me now. I could see things that no one else could see; I could walk into dimensions that were folded inside the real, like the secret vistas in my mother's Hall of Mirrors. Suddenly I thought of that tiny country far away, 'buried in the mountains'. I thought of sheaves of wild flowers in the spring, moonlight on the snowy plains between the ranges, wild horses racing under a violet-tinted moon. I could smell the cold brilliance of the air. I wanted to be there, to fly, to whirl away into the clouds . . .

But my mother says *Take it slowly*, and she's right. I've been only half alive for fourteen years. There's a long and a strange way for me to go before I can be all of myself. So I didn't fly away. Instead I took the little Hindu figure of Ganesh from my pocket and put it on the ground, as near as I could guess to where the altar-niche had been in the sunken room. I'd tell Dita what I'd done with it. I thought she would approve. She'd have to give me another good-luck charm. Maybe I'd even have the courage to give *her* a present this year . . .

And then I walked away down Roman Road, leaving Ganesh there, Lord of Beginnings, to guard the lost gateway into night.

When I was a little boy, I used to have nightmares. When my mother came to comfort me she used to tell me: *You can take control of the bad dream. It's your dream; don't be afraid of it. If it comes again, you take charge. Make it work out all right.* I used to want to be ordinary, like the rest of the world. Now I know that the world is more strange than I could ever have believed possible, and I am part of the strangeness. We've taken control of the wild dream, Mum and Elsa and I, and Mum's advice has worked. It isn't a nightmare any longer.

But the difference is, we are never going to wake up. This dream is real.